INVERSION

NOT YOUR ORDINARY STORIES

BY PAUL STANSBURY

First Edition
2017

Sheppard Press

Sheppard Press
461 Boone Trail
Danville, Kentucky 40422

Printed in the United States of America
ISBN 978-0-9986516-3-7 paperback
ISBN 978-0-9986516-4-4 e-book

Cover Graphics by Paul Stansbury

CONTENTS

INTRODUCTION

INVERSION - NOT YOUR ORDINARY STORIES, is all about speculative fiction. From my viewpoint, this form of fiction places us in a world where the *Laws*, those regularly occurring or apparently inevitable phenomenon that govern what happens to us, operate differently than what we would expect. In the speculative fiction world, the rules as we know them do not always apply. Or could it be the rules as we thought we knew them?

Speculative fiction aims to explore our world as it would be altered by posing the question *What if?* The most appealing and freeing aspect of speculative fiction is that, like the worlds it creates, it is not bound by the traditional genres of Science Fiction, Fantasy, and Horror. In fact it is not bound by any genre. It is free to adventure anywhere it likes as long as anywhere is a creation of imagination and speculation.

INVERSION means turning upside down or inside out; reversal of a normal order or relation. What better title for a collection of speculative fiction stories? When you ask *What if?*, the result is not your ordinary story.

Some of these stories have been previously published, either in print or on line. They have been identified throughout. I wish to express my appreciation to those editors who were willing to publish my work and encourage the reader to visit these other publications.

I would also like to thank the members of the Danville Writers Group, who have read many preliminary drafts of these stories and offered their feedback and assistance.

Finally, I would like to thank Joan Stansbury, affectionately known as the *Queen of Commas*, for her editorial assistance.

Paul Stansbury

UNDER THE WOLF MOON[1]

". . . Mid-Winter's harsh winds and thick snows are perilous for those whose lives depend on the hunt. The moon that rises over the frozen, snow-clad land is called the Hunger Moon because of the gnawing pain brought on by empty hearths. The Indians say they are under the Wolf Moon for it is the time when wolves, driven by hunger, howl through the night outside their villages. Survival often depends on strange and precarious alliances. So it is in this deepest winter. . ."

- From the Diary of Ylva Hemming, Montana Territory
January 9, 1887

* * *

Ylva watched Rollin as he stared out the window across the snow-laden valley. He hunched down on the rough-hewn bench, face inches away from the icy glass. It was an exceptionally hard and bitter winter. Small mounds of powdery snow collected on the floor at the bottom of the cabin door, driven in by a relentless wind. His breath froze instantly on the window's thin panes, requiring him to wipe it away with the warmth of his hands.

"I see them!" he shouted, jumping up from the bench and flinging the door open. He leapt out onto the porch, hand shading his eyes from the brilliant light that glimmered off the snow. A savage gust of wind whirled about the cabin, sucking out what meager warmth the fireplace could force out. "The Hunters are coming."

---

[1] "Under The Wolf Moon" appeared in *Nocturnal Natures A Zimbell House Publishing Anthology* published by Zimbell House Publishing, 9/2016.

"Close that door," Anders bellowed, rising from the table at the back of the cabin. "Have you got no sense you fool? You're letting the death of cold in." He grabbed Rollin by the collar and pulled him back in, slamming the door behind. Then, he peered out of the window.

"There," Rollin pointed, "across the valley – just at the crest of Loup Ridge. Do you see them?"

"Just tricks the sun is playing. Nothing more than shadows from a few rocks," came Ander's gruff reply. "Now don't be opening that door again unless it's to bring in some wood for the fire."

Rollin turned toward Ylva with a plaintive look.

"Mama, you can see them can't you?"

Ylva focused her gray eyes on the distant notch in the ridge that separated their valley from the foothills beyond. There, three figures, dark against the white snow, had just started their descent into the valley. The winter before Rollin was born, she had come down from the distant mountains through that very pass and across the wide valley seeking shelter. They would reach the cabin by midafternoon.

"We'll know soon enough," she replied. "The Hunters always come on the full moon. Now, go and bring in more wood for the fire."

Rollin pulled on a thick coat and thrust his long fingers into a pair of well-worn deerskin gloves. A soft growth of hair flowed down his jaws forming a dark shadow around his lips. He had grown tall and lanky through the summer and now stood as tall as Anders. In all other respects though, he resembled his mother with her finely chiseled features and piercing gray eyes. Ylva watched as he slipped through the door. He stood for a brief moment, peering out across the valley in the direction of the ridge

2

and then sprang from the porch into the yard and bounded through the heavy snow to the woodpile.

"He's becoming quite a man," Anders offered, breaking the brief silence. "Already better at hunting than me and strong for his age."

"Anders, remember he is not you," Ylva said, with a tone of resolution that could not be resisted.

"Well, he's not a boy, just look at him!"

"No, not a boy either."

Anders glared at her. His ruddy cheeks glowed with anger so palpable that it filled her with each breath she took. Over the years, his hatred of the Hunters had grown. As each winter deepened, so did his mood, until he spent the days in sullen silence, dreading their appearance

"They will be here soon," she offered, knowing that the frozen anger of resentment engulfed Anders as completely as the snow covered all the world outside their small cabin.

"By God in heaven, I won't have it - not this year or any year!" Anders bellowed, pounding his fist into the table. "I'll shoot them dead before they set foot in this house."

"And then what," Ylva questioned, knowing she had to choose her words wisely. "How will we survive? How will you keep the cattle and sheep safe as they graze the fields? How will you protect the crops? Without the Hunters, our herds will be ravaged and the crops ruined. What then?"

"Rollin and I can manage."

"But that is the point, there won't be the two of you."

Anders pounded his fist once again. "Enough, I won't suffer any talk of that!"

"But hear it you will," Ylva barked back. "Have you forgotten that I too am born of Hunter stock. Do you not remember the winter before Rollin was born? How I came alone and starving over that very ridge," she pleaded, pointing to the snow clad hills across the valley, "through the bitter wind and chilling snow to this cabin? Fenris had died and without him, I could not hunt enough to survive let alone renew our alliance with you. The summer before, your wife had been taken by the fever. So you and I struck an accord. I have lived up to my part of the bargain. I became your wife and bore you a son. You knew this day would come and agreed that he could leave. Now, you must keep your word. You see that he is no longer a child. If he is to fulfill his birthright, a Hunter's birthright, he must leave. His time has come. He will not stay another spring in this house."

"And why should he wish to leave the comfort of his home and the bounty of this farm?"

"Are you so blind you do not see how he looks at the forests and foothills beyond the valley? Sure, he works hard to please you, but you must know that he sees himself as little more than a mule pulling a plow. His heart belongs to the chase. He longs for the hunt.

"Enough, enough!" spewed Anders, raising his hands.

"Rollin was right," parried Ylva. "There are three coming across the valley. One, who was but a bud last year, will surely be in blossom now."

"By God," gasped Anders, "you don't mean that Hunter's whelp?"

"Curb your tongue, man," growled Ylva. "Freki would make a fine mate for Rollin."

"You have betrayed me!"

The sound of footsteps on the wooden planks outside the door brought the conversation to an abrupt halt.

"Hoy! Open up," Rollin shouted, thumping the door with the toe of his boot. "It's plenty cold out here."

Ylva pulled the door open and Rollin lumbered through carrying a massive load of firewood. He dropped to one knee by the hearth and dumped the splits on the floor. She joined him as he stacked the logs against the rough stones of the fireplace. Anders sat glaring at the table. Presently, he stood up, put on his coat, hat and gloves. Then, flung open the door and stomped off toward the barn. Rollin sprang up and shut the door, but not before watching his father trudge across the snow and disappear into the barn.

"Mama, why is he so mad at the Hunters?"

Ylva picked up some stray splinters from the floor with her nimble fingers and tossed them into the fire. "Because he is afraid."

"Of what? They mean us no harm. Don't they protect our herds and our crops in return for the right to hunt our lands and the little bit of meat in the dead of winter when there is nothing to hunt? What's wrong with that? Seems like a fair arrangement to me. What is he afraid of?"

"He is afraid of what every man is afraid of - being beholden to strangers, growing old, dying alone, having no one to carry on his legacy."

"But Mama, he's got you and me."

"We know that, but he doesn't." Ylva paused, looking into Rollin's grey inquisitive eyes. "Come son, our guests will be here soon and we must ready the house. You go to the cellar and fetch some onions, potatoes and carrots, then bring in some beef. Not from the smokehouse, mind you. Some that's been freshly butchered. "She stepped close and kissed Rollin on the cheek. "As for the rest, you will soon understand."

The afternoon passed quickly. Ylva set the table with the plates Ander's first wife had lugged in her hope chest across the wilderness from her home in Kentucky. She had arrived at Ander's farm in 1869 with her hope chest and two twenty-dollar gold pieces. Her father had arranged the marriage through Ander's father, an occasional drinking companion from a neighboring county. She died less than two years later.

Ylva had filled the large iron kettle with vegetables and hung it on the fireplace crane. The meat was mounted on the spitjack. It had been placed so half rested above the heart of the glowing coals while the other hung beyond the edge of the fire. The savory aroma of roasting meat filled the cabin. Rollin had swept the floor and was setting out forks when Anders burst through the door. He wobbled over to the fire and slumped heavily in his chair, a jug of whisky cradled in his arms. Rollin looked at his father and then at Ylva. She raised her hand signaling him to say nothing, then nodded toward the window. Rollin stepped over and looked out. Their guests were just passing through the fence gate.

"Mama, they're here."

Ylva and Rollin stood at the window watching the three figures cross the snowy yard between the barn and the house. Rollin recognized Hrolf and Ulfa immediately. They had come for many winters. Last year, they had come with their young daughter, Freki. Rollin had guessed her to be about seven or eight years old. Now, a young woman walked with them. His heart raced. Surely, this could not be Freki; but if not, who?

"Anders, our guests are here," Ylva called back over her shoulder. "Please come and welcome them to the house."

Anders spit in the fire. Rollin watched Hrolf come up the steps, pause, then knock at the door.

"Anders, someone, either our guests or you will be sleeping in the barn tonight," Ylva snarled, "Who shall it be?"

Anders snorted, struggled out of his chair and slowly walked over to the door. Ylva wrestled the whisky crock from his arms and wiped his sweaty face with the corner of her apron. His bleary eyes burned holes in the door. Hrolf knocked again. Anders tugged the latch and slowly pulled the door open. The wind whistled through the opening, showering Rollin with a freezing mist of white powder. The hinges groaned in protest. Hrolf stood at the threshold, filling the space with his lanky body. His long sandy colored hair whipped around his hollow cheeks, and his loose clothing flapped on his arms and legs like seed sacks on a fencepost. His fierce, gray-blue eyes did not blink as he stared first at Anders and then at Rollin.

"May this house always have a fire in the hearth and food in the kettle," Hrolf offered.

Anders stood motionless for a moment, eyes glazed with hatred, then hissed, "May your hunt always be successful. " He then turned and returned to his chair.

Ylva stepped forward extending her hand, "Please come in and warm yourselves. Supper will be ready soon and we can talk at the table."

Hrolf motioned for Ulfa and the young woman to come forward. As they reached the door, Hrolf stepped aside, allowing them to enter the house.

"You remember Ulfa," he said, as the older woman entered.

Ulfa smiled. She, like Hrolf, was long limbed. Her thin hands drew back the hood of her simple cape. Rollin found her features as fine as his mother's. Long black hair, stippled with gray, framed a hunter's-tan face. Delicate lines, weatherworn without being rough, emanated from the corners of her pale eyes.

"And this is Freki."

The young woman pulled back the hood of her cape as she stepped to the threshold. She had her mother's face, but her skin, not yet burnished by a life of hunting, was fresh and glowing. Her piercing eyes, however, belonged to Hrolf. The sunlight, seeking its way into the dim cabin, shone through her tousled hair reminding Rollin of the butterfly milkweed's wispy, silvery, seed threads.

Before Rollin had a chance to say anything, Hrolf stepped in and grabbed his hand in a vise-like grip. He clapped Rollin on the shoulder and declared, "I see you have come into your own, big and strong. You'll make a good Hunter." A wide smile broke across his face. "So what do you think of our Freki? I think she has grown as beautiful as you have grown strong."

"I. . . I," stammered Rollin.

"Yes, I agree."

Rollin looked at Freki. Crimson flushed her cheeks as she turned her eyes away.

"Please come to the fire and warm yourselves," Ylva invited, as she gathered their cloaks. "Supper will be ready soon and we have much to discuss." She ushered them to the hearth. Rollin took the cloaks from his mother and hung them on the wall pegs behind the door.

Anders sat slumped in his chair, staring at the glowing embers under the kettle. The odor of stewing vegetables and roasting meat did little to brighten his spirit. Hrolf, Ulfa and Freki huddled to the far side of the hearth, giving him wide berth. Ylva swung the kettle out from the fire and stirred the vegetables with a worn, wooden spoon. She reached for a small box from the mantle above and doused the mixture with a pinch of salt. She returned the kettle to its spot in the glowing firebox, then took a poker and rotated the meat on the spitjack. Drippings sizzled and burst into flame as they fell onto the embers below.

"Rollin, finish setting the table," Ylva coaxed. "Freki, would you care to help?"

"Yes, Freki," declared Ulfa, "go help Rollin. I'm sure he would favor your company." Freki sidled up to Rollin. She brought the warmth of the fire with her. An ephemeral fragrance of moss and mayflowers filled his head. His heart raced. "The plates are in the press," he panted, suddenly short of breath. Although the cabin was none too warm, he could feel beads of sweat forming on his forehead. He hurried off in the direction of the cupboard. Freki moved with him step for step. His heart settled down as he gently placed the plates in her waiting hands. They continued to busy themselves setting the table, oblivious to their surroundings. Anders dozed in his chair, shifting occasionally with a snort. The others had moved to the far side of the cabin sitting on low stools, heads bowed furtively in deep discussion.

"I must get some fresh water," Rollin said, slipping a long arm into his coat sleeve. "I'll be right back." Freki placed her hand on his arm while she reached for her cloak. "You needn't go out in the cold," he said. She pulled up her hood and smiled. "Oh, alright." He smiled and opened the door. The sun was just touching the ridge across the valley. Amber light bathed the snow-clad landscape. Freki slipped her arm through the bend in Rollin's elbow, pressing her body close to his. They walked on silently until they reached the cistern. Freki helped Rollin pull aside two of the cover planks. He filled the bucket with water. As he finished replacing the planks, he felt an icy tingle on his neck.

He straightened up and a freezing cold glob of snow slid down his back. Freki squealed with laughter as Rolling shuddered. She threw a handful of snow in his face then dashed off toward the cabin with him in pursuit. He didn't catch up with her until they reached the porch. She reeled around, eyes flashing. A wide smile spread across her face. Rollin stopped, his face just inches away from hers. The last of the snow melted and trickled down his spine, sending shivers through his body. She gently wiped the wet snow from his face. Her hands were warm and soft against his cold skin. He opened his mouth but no words would come out. She touched her fingers to his lips.

"You forgot the water," she gleefully chuckled, pointing to the bucket sitting by the cistern. Rollin looked over his shoulder in exasperation. When he looked back, she had disappeared through the door.

Everyone was seated by the time he retrieved the bucket.

"Put some wood on the fire." Anders rasped, taking a long drink from his cup. Rollin set the bucket down by the dry sink. The meat had been removed from the spitjack and was sitting on a platter in front of Anders, waiting to be carved. The kettle rested on a trivet at the other end of the table. After tossing some splits into the hearth, Rollin sat down at his place between Anders and Ylva. The only sound to be heard was the pop and crackle of the fire.

They sat silent heads bowed until Ylva said, "Anders, the food is getting cold."

"May your hunt always be successful," muttered Anders.

"May this house always have a fire in the hearth and food in the kettle," Hrolf responded.

They fell into silence once again. "Our guests would prefer their meat cut from the left," Ylva offered, referring to the meat that had not been roasted directly over the coals. Anders took up the bone handled carving knife in one hand and used the other to skewer the roast with a long fork. He hacked away at the roast as if he were stabbing a wild animal. Soon, rough slabs of meat were slapped on plates and passed to the Hunters. He turned to the other end and cut slices for Ylva and Rollin. Vegetables were passed along with thick slices of freshly baked bread. Anders took no food on his plate. Rather, he filled his cup with more whisky and kept a tight grip on the carving knife throughout the meal, all the while glaring at the Hunters.

Between bites, Rollin watched the Hunters. The way they ate, Rollin thought they must not have eaten in days. They attacked their food, cutting the nearly raw meat into thick chunks, sopping up the red juice in the bottom of their plates with the bread. The coppery smell of blood filled his nostrils and he had to resist the urge to snatch up a glistening chunk of meat and shove it in his watering mouth.

Night had descended by the end of the meal. Rollin could see the last of the full moon just rising as he carried the dirty dishes to the dry sink. After the table had been cleared, he filled a kettle with water and placed it on the fireplace crane to warm. He returned to his place at the table. They sat in silence for some time. Then Hrolf reached inside his shirt. Anders clutched the carving knife to his chest.

"You have no need for that," Hrolf gestured to the knife. He pulled a clenched hand from his shirt. Slowly, he opened his fingers, revealing a large bear claw. "This we bring you as fulfillment of our pledge and in promise of our service to this house." He laid the bear claw on the table before Anders.

"That means nothin' to me," bellowed Anders, sweeping the bear claw away with the back of his hand. You could have found that anywhere."

"That is so; but, perhaps this will convince you otherwise," snarled Hrolf, pulling open his shirt. Four ragged scars ran from neck to waist. Ylva gasped.

"So be it," Anders huffed. He laid the knife on the table, its tip pointed at Hrolf. "Say what you've come to say and be done with it."

"As you wish. As has been the practice between our races, we come to renew our compact. Our fathers and their fathers lived in peace and benefited from this alliance. So it has been and should continue between us. In this land, there is room for both to live. Like you, we ask for little but to follow the traditions of our ancestors. Each of us in our own way lives from the land. You tend your herds and plow the earth. We hunt. We ask only to freely hunt your fields. We will take only what we need. In return, we will protect your livestock from predators and your crops from foragers."

"Is that all?" Anders asked.

"Only that when the land lies frozen and snow covers the fields, the kindness of some meat to carry us through to Spring."

"Well now ain't that a fine story," Anders bellowed, slamming his hand on the table. "The mighty Hunters, starving and shivering in the snow, come a beggin' to the poor, helpless farmer. 'Oh, please give us some meat and we'll catch some field mice for you.' By God, a good rat snake can do that for me, and I don't have to invite him to supper!"

Hrolf jumped up from his seat, leaning across the table. He looked straight into Anders bleary eyes and growled, "Break the alliance, and you'll find it hard to plow a straight row looking over your shoulder."

"And what's that supposed to mean?" Anders spumed.

"Enough!" Ylva protested. "Alcohol is no substitute for common sense," she hissed, "and threats benefit none of us!" Hrolf sat down, glaring at Anders. She walked around the table and picked up the bear claw from its resting place near the hearth. The light from the embers glowed red in the fissures and grooves of the curved barb. "Surely, this bear was a fierce warrior and a deadly foe," she pronounced, taking up a position up behind Anders. "We are honored," she said, addressing Hrolf. "You have bravely kept your pledge and we humbly accept your protection." She jabbed the claw into Ander's ribs. "In return, we invite you to hunt our fields and in time of need take that which you need, don't we, husband."

"Aye," he muttered under his breath. "If that's the way it's to be."

"That's the way it will be," she bristled.

Ulfa, placed her hand on Hrolf's arm. "And we are grateful to this house for the generosity and humbly accept your offer, don't we, husband?" Her fingers clamped his flesh like a steel trap.

"Yes," Hrolf grumbled.

Ylva returned to her seat at the table. They sat in silence. Moonlight poured through the window above the dry sink as the candles on the table burned low. The night winds gusted, causing the window panes to rattle. Sparks from the dying fire whirled up the chimney as burning logs crumbled in the hearth.

Finally, Ylva looked at Ulfa, who nodded in silent response, releasing her hold on Hrolf's arm. Standing, she said,

"The Moon rises. We have little time and must make ready our journey home."

Anders sloshed more whisky in his cup. Then, without looking up, awkwardly waved his hand in the air, blurting out, "Good! Go. Leave my house. Take whatever you want. But, do it now. Leave me alone. Go."

"Yes, it's better if you leave the house now," Ylva said, getting up from table. "But take some time to rest in the barn before you go."

They left Anders, head bowed, at the table. Ylva, Hrolf and Ulfa huddled beside the door whispering, while Rollin helped Freki with her cloak. As he finished tying the lace of her hood, she pressed her body close to his and gently nuzzled his cheek. Her hot breath spilled down his neck as his trembling fingers caressed her face.

Hrolf clapped Rollin on the shoulder and leaned in close. "No time for that now, you two. Maybe later, aye?"

"I. . . I," stammered Rollin.

"You say that quite a lot. Come, Freki, we must make ready."

Rollin stood still, feet nailed to the floor planks, as the three Hunters slipped out the door. Looking through the window, he followed their black silhouettes until they disappeared into the barn.

"Come, son," Ylva beckoned, "help me clear away this mess."

They cleared the table, making sure not to disturb Anders. Ylva kept a watchful eye on his cup, making sure that it stayed full. The dishes were washed and placed back on the shelves above the dry sink and the kettle was oiled and set by the hearth. Rollin swept the floor, tossing the crumbs on the embers in the hearth. He watched his mother pour more whisky into his father's large cup. He had never seen his father drink so heavily, nor his mother so willingly encourage him. Soon, Anders' head fell none too softly on the table. Ylva cleared away the whisky and sat heavily in her rocker by the fire. Rollin watched as she wearily threw some wood in the glowing mouth of the hearth. She turned in his direction and said, "To bed."

"Mama?"

Ylva held up a hand to signal that she had no conversation left in her. He slowly climbed the ladder to the loft where he slept and slumped into the old canvass tick stuffed with straw that served as his bed. Save for the occasional snort from Anders, the cabin fell silent. Rollin was pleased to sleep in the loft during the long winter. Heat from the fireplace rose up and hung about the rafters just above his head, protecting him from the chill drafts that whisked through below. He wondered how Hrolf, Ulfa, and Freki were faring in the barn.

Rollin soon fell into a fretful sleep. He dreamed it was night and he was running through the woods. The moon drifted in and out of the clouds, its light filtering down through the leafy canopy. The heady essence of the forest filled him until he thought his lungs would burst. As he ran, he became aware of a new scent, subtle but compelling, intriguingly woven in with the usual fare the forest offered up. His heart pounded with feral passion as he drank it into his heaving lungs. He glimpsed lupine silhouettes running with him step for step. Ahead, he could see a single she-wolf. Her lithe body seemed to float across the forest floor compared to his awkward thrashing. Long hair flowing, she looked back at him, eyes flashing. Try as he might, he could not catch her. He thought his lungs would burst. His legs ached. Stumbling, he fell to the ground, arms and legs akimbo. He laid on the cool leaves, eyes shut, while he waited for the spinning in his head to stop. Opening his eyes, he found the she-wolf standing over him. His lungs heaved, sucking in deep breaths flavored with moss and mayflowers. As the moon peeked out from behind a cloud, the she-wolf's face melted away. Freki smiled, moonlight glimmering over her bare shoulders. She leaned in close. Her hot breath spilled over his heaving chest as he reached up with trembling hands. . .

"Rollin, wake up," Ylva coaxed, gently nudging his shoulder. He opened his eyes as she placed her hand to his lips. Her fingers were cold and he could see snow melting on the hood of her cloak. "Shhhh," she whispered, "get dressed and meet me in the barn, and don't wake your father."

"Mama?"

"Enough," she chided. "The moon rises high in the sky."

She slipped down the ladder heading to the door of the cabin. Rollin heard the swish of the wind as the door opened. He scrambled down from the loft. He quickly dressed while Anders snored softly at the table. A cold blast of air hit his face as he cracked the door open. The night wind gusted as he stepped on the porch. Drift snow crunched under his boot heels. The last of the full moon bathed everything in pale blue. Rollin made his way to the barn. He could hear his mother and the Hunters talking in low tones as he opened the door. In dim lantern light, Ylva and the Hunters were busily dividing portions of cured meat into four bundles.

"There he is," Ylva declared. "Come here, son," she commanded, "we have much to discuss and little time left. "

"Mama?"

"Questions later. For now, you must listen." Rollin joined the group, sitting next to his mother. "I am sorry I did not tell you this sooner, but I feared you might have said something which would cause your father to spoil your chance. You must listen carefully, for your future is at hand. You know that I am born of Hunters and therefore you, as my son, are born of Hunters. It is a birthright that no one, not even your father, can deny.

"Men can only see Hunters as they are now when the full moon rises in the dead of Winter. Only then do Hunters enter the realm of men. For when the full moon has passed, Hunters return to their true form, once again running free and wild. And so your birthright demands the same of you. Tonight, you must leave your human form and take your place among the Hunters. I fear you have no choice. As a child, you kept the form of men, but now that you are no longer a child, you must put away that which you cling to as a child and take up your birthright as a Hunter. What waits for you will be unlike anything you have experienced. Your journey will be frightening but beautiful beyond your dreams. You will not be alone, for Hrolf, Ulfa and Freki will be with you."

"But, what of you, Mama?" Rollin asked. "You say you were born of Hunters, yet you have stayed."

"Yes, Ylva," Hrolf added, "What of you? Your obligation has been met, come hunt with us again."

"No, I cannot return," Ylva replied, voice cracking. " Anders and I struck our accord the night I came to his door, the night I conceived his child." She placed her hand on Rollin's shoulder. "You, whose time has come. But, as for me, because the full moon had not passed, I was trapped in this form, destined to remain in human form until the end of my days. "

"And what of Rollin," asked Ulfa, "how can you be sure that he will not suffer the same fate as you? Would you have us take him only to find out that he too must remain like you? We would find that most unsuitable."

"Last winter, after you left, Rollin fell ill, racked with pain until Spring. It was no fever or sickness. He was struggling to change but not yet strong enough to cast off the shackles of his human form. But now he is ready. This time, he will change, if only to be with Freki." Ylva smiled. "Although he might not yet be willing to admit it."

"And what of Freki," asked Hrolf, turning to his daughter. "What say you? Will you have Rollin here?"

"Yes."

Ylva touched Rollin's face. "Do not be afraid. As you have dreamt, so it shall come to pass."

Rollin's heart leapt. "Now, I may go freely and gladly, no matter what consequence awaits. And although I am uncertain of all that lies ahead, I believe it is the path I must follow." He looked at Ylva. "But what of you and Papa? I wish not to desert you. And surely this will sit ill with him."

Ylva smiled. "Our children are meant to make their own way, to follow their own path. You are a Hunter. You will form your own alliances and teach your offspring the way of the Hunters. But, you will not forget us; and perhaps, in the Spring, you will leave a hare at the door for our kettle. I will see to your father.

"Now, all that is settled, we must hurry. Load the meat on the small sledge. It will be easier to pull across the snow than trying to carry by hand. Anders can retrieve it tomorrow."

After everything was packed, the Hunters and Rollin set out on their journey across the valley. Ylva stood on the cabin porch for a long time, watching them trudge through the snow pulling the sledge. By the time the moon reached the jagged horizon, they had become tiny dark specks silhouetted against the moon just before it dipped behind the rocks. She blew out her oil lamp and slipped inside.

Rollin stood at the crest of Loup Ridge. He looked back across the valley one last time. The cabin he had called home looked small and strangely unfamiliar in the moonlight. Just before he turned, the pinpoint of light he had watched throughout the night disappeared.

Ylva sat in her rocker, occasionally nudging the logs with the poker. Pale sunlight soon drifted in through the windows. She brewed fresh coffee and cut some thick slices of bread from the last night's loaf. She was pondering whether or not to rouse Anders when he raised his head from the table.

"Have they gone?" he rasped.

"Yes."

"Good. Where's Rollin?" he asked, looking around.

"He's not here, he left with the Hunters."

"By God," Anders bellowed, "I thought I told you no!"

"It wasn't your choice, it was his to make.

"Not if I have anything to say about it."

"Well, you don't. There's nothing you can do now. He's made up his mind and that's all there is to it."

"We'll see about that!"

Anders snatched up his jug and took a long draught of whisky, then pulled his rifle down from the rack above the fireplace, stuffing a handful of cartridges in his pocket. He grabbed up his hat and coat, flung open the door and disappeared into the sunlight.

* * *

Anders returned late in the afternoon as the sun bathed the snow-clad valley in an amber hue. Frost caked his beard. His coat, thick with ice, refused to relinquish its cold grip. Ylva helped him pull off his gloves and boots and he slumped wearily into his chair by the fire.

Ylva mixed some whisky in a tankard of hot coffee and handed it to Anders. "Did you find them?" she asked.

Anders stared blankly into the embers of the fire. "Gone. Followed their tracks up to Loup Ridge. Found the sledge at the base. From there, followed their tracks right up to a shallow cave just below the notch - not much more than a crack in the rock. Boot prints going in, bare feet coming out. Found their clothes tucked in a notch at the back. About half of the meat was buried in the snow. Followed the footprints up a ways to the crest. Only found wolf tracks on the other side."

Ylva knelt down beside Anders. "It's what was meant to be. All your life, you've been able to bend most things to your will, this land, me. I sometimes think you can even make the weather do what you want. But, you can't bend everything to your will. You can't hold on to anything forever. This was one of those things beyond you. You'll just have to accept it. You had him for a right smart time - a lifetime for many. But now it's his time, and Freki's time. You've got to let them go."

* * *

". . . It has been three years since Anders passed. This morning, I found two hares at the front door - a farewell present from Rollin and Freki. They must have come a far piece to bring them. Everything is packed. Must remember to tell the new owners about the Hunters. I do not know how I will manage living in town. Survival always depends on strange and precarious alliances . . ."

- From the Diary of Ylva Hemming, Montana Territory
May 20, 1892

A PASSAGE ON THE CALEUCHE

Janic woke up assaulted by his senses. The light, the sounds, the odors around him were exquisitely vivid almost to the point they were painful. He lifted himself up on one arm, his equilibrium immediately distorted. *Give it time.*

"Better give it some time," said the face of his shipmate, Briggs, from the monitor. "Acclimation takes a while. Everyone experiences it differently. Best sit still while you get your bearings."

"Are we there?" Janic asked, pushing himself into a sitting position. He could feel his hair just brushing the top of the capsule.

"Hardly."

"Why be pulled out then?"

"Ours is not to reason . . ."

"Yeah, yeah, I know." Janic surveyed the space inside his cocoon. His identification badge and wallet lay on a small ledge at his side. Beneath that, was an array of touch controls to manage the amenities of his little world.

"You'll be wanting to bathe once you get your sea legs," Briggs continued. "The lavatory is at the end of the corridor to your right as you exit your rabbit hole."

"Funny."

"Knock first, it's unisex. You'll find a fresh coverlet there. At the other end, you'll find the Mess and Common, which, by the way, has a spectacular view of our destination." The monitor blinked off.

* * *

Once he felt steady, Janic touched the appropriate control and the opaque plasma door at his feet melted away. He wormed out of the opening until he could sit up, feet dangling over the edge. He stuck his head into the long corridor and looked around. *I don't recall the GSS Eurydice being large enough to hold quarters this size.* His capsule was situated in the second tier. His toes were just a few inches from the deck. *Thank goodness, what in the hell was I going to do if I was at the top? I doubt my legs could handle such a drop.* He eased out, bracing himself with his elbows until he was sure his legs could handle his weight.

Janic had just finished toweling off and was pulling his coverlet on when Briggs's face appeared in the lavatory mirror. "Jeez," Janic panted, "you startled me. I didn't think they had this kind of set up on a patrol ship."

"They don't. I wanted to let you settle in a bit before breaking the news. After we took off, we were transferred to the MT Caleuche."

"I don't recognize the designation 'MT'."

"Meta-Transport."

"I've never heard of that."

"Neither had I. My guess is it's one of those 'eyes only' things."

"I don't understand, under what authority do they do such a thing?"

"Who can fathom the mysteries of God, much less those in charge?" The screen melted back into Janic's reflection.

"Wait! I have more questions." Janic shouted to his reflection. *Dammit Briggs.* He waited, hoping Briggs would reappear. Only his own, drawn countenance stared back at him. *Maybe I should go to the Common. There's bound to be someone there who can fill me in on what's happening. Damn that Briggs,*

22

he can be such an ass. He drifted down the corridor past the rows of stacked cubicles. In addition to a name plaque, each door had a number preceded by 'CC' above its door. *Looks like I'm in section CC.* He examined the names as he moved along. *I wish there was at least one name along here I recognize. There are quite a few of us who signed on the Eurydice together. Where is Briggs berthed, I wonder? Why didn't he come to fetch me in person?* Janic passed through the bulkhead, entering a fair sized vestibule. The uncomfortably jumbled odor of highly processed food wafted out through the portal on his left, identifying the location of the Mess. To his right was an nondescript bulkhead. Straight ahead through a wide portal, he could see a large room filled with chairs and lounges. This must be the Common. He stepped forward.

The enclosure was generous for a space-going vessel. The semicircular deck was enclosed by a clear wall of plasma which started at deck level, arching upward and around to a height of two full decks above his head. Outside, he could clearly see the star-filled expanse of the universe. He walked into the room. It was like standing on the top of a mountain on a clear moonless night. Music of indeterminate style, loud enough to be annoying, clattered about the room. To Janic's dismay, he could see only a single individual, seated on a lounge close to the juncture of plasma windows and the deck. He was wearing a drab coat over a dingy, collarless white shirt, buttoned, old fashion style, right up to the neck. His trousers were worn and stained. *What an odd get-up.* Janic made a beeline to the shabby man.

Janic was about to speak when the shabby man said, "Aye t'was bitter cold."

"Bitter cold?" Janic repeated the shabby man's words. *This is weird.*

"Aye, I remember. Deep in the ship, t'was hot from the bodies and the steam. But outside, in the black void with only the stars for light, t'was bitter cold. A man can't last long in the sea of despair and freezing cold. Where you shippin' out from laddie?"

Sounds like a Scot "I was transferred here from the GSS Eurydice, out of the lunar base in Mare Vaporum. Without my knowledge I might add. Do you know –."

"There was a fellow here just a bit ago who was on the Ourang Medan. Had a frightful time, according to him. As for me, I shipped out from Southampton on the –."

"I don't mean to interrupt, sir, but do you know where I can find someone in charge?"

"Well, but you have interrupted me. So it appears you're too important to pass the time with steerage. But if it's any matter to ye, try talking to that there," the shabby man said pointing to the low table in front of a chair across the way. "Went to put me feet up," he said looking around, "and seein' no badges about, had just touched me boot heel to the edge when a mirror popped up and some feller that wasn't me started talkin'. I'd seen him in some other mirrors around the boat. Well, I beat it over here before he could see me an' soon enough the thing disappeared."

Strange. Janic walked over and sat down in the chair. He looked at the low table. It had a set of touch controls and a screen on its surface. *Nothing ventured.* He reached out, but before he could activate the screen, it flipped up.

"I see you found the Common," Briggs said.

Finally. "Briggs, please, you've got to tell me what's going on. Nothing makes sense."

"Of course it does. You're still a bit muddled from the stasis."

"At least tell me why we were transferred to this ship?" pleaded Janic.

"That's simple, because the Eurydice is gone."

"Gone?" Janic gasped. "This can't be!"

"Yes it can, we had just initiated our jump orbit around Wolf 359 in route to the Triangulum when we were caught in an unexpected solar ejecta of unprecedented magnitude. We came here while the Eurydice became so much star fodder."

"So what now? Do we have orders? Are they sending a ship to pick us up?"

"We have a destination."

"Where?" Janic asked, as the screen flipped down. *Briggs, you bastard, you can't do that to me.* He frantically poked the screen activator to no avail. *What's happening? This can't be protocol even for a rescue mission.* He turned to ask the shabby man another question. He was no where to be seen. Janic quickly looked around the lounge. He was alone. *Something's wrong. There should be others here – others who could help me understand what is happening to me.* He stood up and faced the plasma windows. The two story sweep of windows filled his field of vision. *So many stars. So many more than I could ever see from Earth's polluted atmosphere. No navigating by the constellations this far in deep space. Infinite, flowing out forever. What's that? Pale reflections in the plasma. People behind me, staring out of the window, just like me.* He whirled around to face an empty room. *Get ahold of yourself. Gotta be aftereffects of stasis. Maybe they botched it, Maybe my brains are scrambled.* He turned his attention back to the window.

"There 'tis, dead ahead," said a voice beside him.

Janic craned his head to the left to see the shabby man now standing along side. *What the hell?*

"Right there," the shabby man pointed upward, finger almost touching the plasma. "See it? The soft one. Not a harsh light like all those stars out there, burning their souls away. No, the one with the soft light, the Pearl of Creation."

Briggs' face materialized on the plasma surface. "He's right you know, it's the Pearl of Creation. That's where we're going – now that you're here. We've been waiting for you."

What's goin on? Janic reached toward Briggs' image. *This is just too crazy. Why have I never heard of that star?* The image dissolved, replaced once again the by the faces, each staring at the Pearl which was now aligned in the center of his own reflection. *It's getting bigger by the second.*

"Aye, we have been waitin' laddie," the shabby man continued, "and dead ahead is the Pearl of Creation, where all the energy of the universe was let go in an instant at the beginning and it's been trying to get back there ever since. Whether 'tis a lowly worm or the largest galaxy, when it dies, goes back there. I'm goin' there and you're goin' there – when your turn comes. 'Tis no escapin' it. 'Till then, ye mus' tell it to those who book passage on the Caleuche. An' when the last berth is filled, then comes your turn."

"But, why me?"

"I don't know the answer to that one, laddie. Jus' stay the course and your time will come," said the shabby man. He reached his hand up and out to the plasma window and moved forward. "Yes, it's cold," he said, as hand passed through. The tips of his fingers streamed away toward the Pearl in wispy tendrils, followed by his hand as he rose from the deck. Janic watched as he disappeared through the widow, the thin mist of his being stretching out of sight. *My God.* The faces now took their form, passing through the plasma into the void, rising like the smoke prayers of the ancients to the heavens.

The other passengers, his shipmates from the Eurydice among them, filed past in silence, inexorably drawn into the Pearl of Creation. Its pull on him grew until he though he would surely be ripped away. Finally, Briggs appeared at his side.

"Don't worry Janic," he said. "You took the last birth. I died a split second before you otherwise I would be staying. All who perish at sea, whether on earth or in the vast ocean of the universe, like us, must berth on the Caleuche before moving on. When it reaches port, whoever has the last berth must stay for the next voyage, to guide the new passengers. Don't worry, you will be first ashore when next the Caleuche sails this way."

The Pearl of Creation now dwarfed the Caleuche, its insatiable thirst devouring the roiling spirits, Janic threw up his arms as if to fend off the impending collision.

* * *

The Common was filled with passengers. Janic sat on the lounge close to the juncture of plasma windows, staring out into the star-filled expanse of the Universe. Waiting, longing. He was wearing his scorched duty uniform. A woman, like all the others before her, entered through the portal at the far end. She frantically searched the room. Empty to her eyes, save for Janic. He turned his head. Once she made eye contact, she hurried over to where he sat.

"It was fiercely hot," he began.

"Fiercely hot?" the woman repeated Janic's words.

"Yes, I remember. Everything was fine inside. But outside, in the blinding glare of the ejecta, it's fiercely hot. A man can't last long in the cauldron of despair and scorching heat. Where were you shipping out from ma'am?"

27

"I was on the Valencia. How and why I got here, I have no idea. Do you know--"

"There was a fellow here just a bit ago who was on the Titanic. Had a frightful time, according to him. As for me, I shipped out from the lunar base in Mare Vaporum on the –."

"I don't mean to interrupt, sir, but do you know where I can find someone in charge?"

CAMERA OBSCURA

"It will take but a moment for your eyes to adjust to the dark. Once that has happened, we can move on to the demonstration," LaBraid offered, pushing the small door closed, shutting out the sunlight.

"Well be quick about it, LaBraid, I am a busy man!"

"Be at ease, Cresil. Just a few adjustments and you will witness a marvel of the optical sciences. I trust you managed to negotiate the tower stairs without mishap. They can be quite treacherous."

"I prefer to be called by my proper title: Monsignor, if you please. We are not childhood familiars anymore," Cresil growled.

"As you wish, Monsignor Cresil, but keep in mind a title and cassock do not a man make. I remember when we played in the courtyard below the rectory. How many years ago? What sway you couldn't get from beguiling lies, you gained through violence and intimidation. You may rely on the same tactics now, but be assured it no longer works with me."

"If you have something to show me, then get on with it, for I have little time or patience for your prattle!"

"Are you familiar with the camera obscura, Monsignor? Perfected by the Persian scientist Alhazen of Basra some eight hundred years ago," asked LaBraid

"No doubt a Muslim heretic!"

"As I was saying, from the Latin 'camera' referring to a chamber, combined with 'obscura' meaning dark. It is one and the same as the darkened chamber in which you now stand. Add a mirror, a few bits of glass, an opening to let in the light, and you have an optical device that projects an image of its surroundings on the table before you."

Cresil reached out tentatively with his hand to touch the large round table. He had only just caught a glimpse of it in the glare of light that had accompanied him when he entered the small unlit cupola. His fingers followed the table's smooth edge. It filled the center of the chamber, leaving only enough room between it and the walls for a person to stand.

"Almost like the confessional, wouldn't you say Monsignor? But, here a priest can't fumble with himself in the dark while school boys describe their impure thoughts."

"Mind your tongue, and remember that you are allowed to remain here only by my grace. Do not confuse this wretched shed atop your filthy quarters with the Holy Church. I have had quite enough of your salacious twaddling. I should like to leave now."

"I am afraid that will have to wait," LaBraid whispered, positioning himself between the door and Cresil. The priestly odor of sweat and stale altar wine filled his nostrils. "I haven't shown you what you need to see. Be still, Monsignor, while we examine what the camera obscura has to offer. All I need do is engage this lever, opening the aperture above. The outside light flowing in will reflect off the mirror I have mounted directly over this table and down through a series of lenses producing the effect you are about to witness."

Cresil gasped as brilliant light poured down from above and reflected up from the smooth white table top, assaulting his eyes. A familiar tableau came into focus.

"This is what you have wasted my time with?" he spewed. "A painting of the town outside your window. This is what you were so anxious to show me? I could have just as easily looked out my own window."

"Look closely, Monsignor Cresil, this is no painting. No, it is something quite different altogether. A painting is simply a representation of what the artist interprets. The camera obscura reflects each moment. Like life itself, it is ever changing; never returning to the moment just past, always progressing to the moment just next. Look there," he ordered, pointing to an area just below the center of the scene laid out before them. "Watch as the hay wagon moves along the street, and here," his finger traced along the street, "a servant girl is entering the butcher shop."

"Blasphemy, the work of the devil!" Cresil blared. "I'll see that this abomination is destroyed and you are banished for the rest of your miserable life."

"For what? Lining up a mirror and a few optical lenses to capture the light and project it down on a board? Simple science. And besides, do you really think the church has that much influence anymore? I doubt it. None-the-less, you'll not leave just now. There is much more to be revealed."

In the reflected light, Cresil could see LaBraid reach over and turn a hand crank. The images on the table began to magnify in concert with the soft squeaking of gears.

"Now, look closely, Monsignor, and you will be able to discern the features of your parishioners. I believe that is the spinster, Miss Morgan, walking along the sidewalk in her usual drab attire, parasol opened to protect her delicate skin from the sun. And there are some of your young acolytes laughing and playing in the same courtyard where we played as youths."

Cresil stood still, eyes fixed on the images that spread out before him. "Chimeras, parlor tricks, LaBraid. This is no séance where you can fool the weak-minded with horns and shaking furniture. You might invite some old widows to your parlor of chicanery, and wrest a few dollars out of their purses with these tricks, but not me!"

"You will find no delusions here, Monsignor," LaBraid protested raising his arm to point in the direction of the rectory. "The place for that is across the way."

"Enough of this," Cresil bellowed. "Let me out before I call for the constable and have you arrested on the spot!"

"You'll be leaving soon enough, but not before I'm ready for you to go. There are still things you need to see." Reaching for the lever, LaBraid closed the aperture in the ceiling, plunging them into darkness once again.

"What now you madman? I will see you spend the rest of your miserable existence in the asylum for this."

"Have you ever heard of a 'Claude glass'? I doubt it. The closed minds of priests won't tolerate any knowledge outside of a catechism. I would expect the same of you. Commonly known as a 'Black Mirror,' it is different than an ordinary mirror such as the one currently mounted in the roof above. Slightly convex, with its surface tinted in a dark color, it has the curious effect of disengaging the subject reflected in it from its surroundings, reducing and simplifying its essence. I found it has a very unique and interesting effect when employed in the camera obscura, as you will soon see."

The muted clatter of machinery above added to his disorientation as Cresil strained to see in the dark. Once again, dazzling light pooled on the table temporarily blinding the priest.

"What now?" he implored.

"Look for yourself. Closer! See what the Black Mirror reveals."

"It looks the same as before. Whatever effect you wanted to create through this parlor trick has failed. Now let me out!"

"Even I am not sure whether the effects of the Black Mirror are mere optics or something more; but they are undeniable. Let us apply more magnification to the image." LaBraid turned the hand crank. Once again, the figures grew larger until their faces were clearly in view. "There," he panted pointing to Miss Morgan, "tell me what you see."

"My God," Cresil gasped as he looked down at the woman, now clothed in a bright red satin dress, cut low to reveal her ample bosom. Her face was slathered in garish makeup in a vain attempt to conceal the wrinkles and crow's feet of her advancing age. She licked her lips invitingly as a young stable hand approached on the sidewalk.

"What matter of sorcery is this, LaBraid? You'll be damned to hell for this abomination!"

"No sorcery involved here, Monsignor, I leave that to the priests and wizards. I have encountered these interesting, yet disturbing, phenomena during many observations. And I have come to the inescapable conclusion that the camera obscura reveals what lies deep within man - those dark propensities we dare not expose in fear of the consequences should they become known. In the case of our Miss Morgan, we see that the prim and proper spinster lusts for the comfort of younger men. No doubt, the stable boy will soon be summoned to her house under the pretext of doing some odd job, only to end up rutting with her in the tool shed."

"Stop!" Cresil pleaded, raising his hands to cover his eyes. "Enough of this salacious trickery."

"Not yet! There is more to reveal than mere dalliances. Now to serious business. We have yet to peel back the veneer of the human soul and gaze upon the most heinous sins. Those perhaps even God cannot forgive."

Cresil, still pressing his hands tightly to his eyes, heard the grinding of gears once again. "Please," he bleated, "stop this now, I can take no more. Let me go and I promise I will say nothing. No harm will come to you or your wretched machine. I promise."

"I thought I had made it clear to you that I am not fooled by the bluster of the Church. You have no power over me and consequently your promises are as hollow and worthless as your office. Now, remove your hands and see what the camera obscura has revealed!"

"No, no. Please let me go."

LaBraid grasped Cresil's left arm in a crushing grip, pulling it away from his face. "Open your eyes or I will tear them from their sockets!"

Cresil dropped his right arm with no further protest and slowly opened his throbbing eyes. The bright, blurred images on the table coalesced into a scene of the court yard outside the rectory. The altar boys he had seen playing just moments before now stood motionless, staring up as if to look into his eyes.

"Do you see, Monsignor Cresil?" LaBraid hissed, pulling the priest's arm closer to the table. "Look at their faces. Drawn, pale, almost translucent, the beauty of innocent youth has been sucked from their souls leaving only fear, hurt, and loathing. Each time they come from the rectory - your rectory, they fade a little more. Sooner or later they become a dried husk, to be crushed under the boot heal of life or blown away by the wind. What abhorrent acts must have occurred behind those walls!"

"I have done nothing wrong. It was not I who sinned," Cresil whimpered. "I know they wanted it, they lured me, God knows I tried to resist."

"Now, who is the blasphemer, the one who justifies his sins in God's name?" LaBraid wrenched the priest's hand down flat on the table. The faces of the altar boys crawled over its pallid skin. In one swift movement, LaBraid drew a knife from his pocket, raised it above his head and brought it down, impaling Cresil's hand. The blade drove deep into the wood underneath. The priest writhed in burning pain as blood welled up from the wound and trickled off in rivulets.

Moaning in agony, Cresil watched in horror as the faces of the altar boys flowed to the blood, greedily lapping up the thick red fluid. Flushed with horror and revulsion, he pulled the knife from his hand and bolted for the door. Flinging it open, he ran out into the blinding light catching his boot heal on the step. He reached for the banister, but his hand, covered in slick blood, could not hold on and he plunged headlong down the steep flights until he landed in a lifeless heap at the bottom. LaBraid descended the stairs and stood in silence until the constable had been summoned.

"Sure 'ad a nasty fall didn't he, Mr. LaBraid," Constable Ferryman said, gently poking the dead priest who lay at the bottom of the tower stairs.

"Indeed he had. The stairs can be quite treacherous."

"What's this 'ere cut on his hand all about?"

"Oh, I'm afraid there is a loose spike on the banister at the top. He must have lost his footing and cut his hand while trying to regain his balance."

"Lost his footing, you say?"

"Yes, lost his footing and that led to his fall. A long fall, longer than you can imagine."

INSTANTANEOUS[2]

Bits of memory flashed amid the pain. He struggled with gauzy phantasms. Rain. Speed. Alcohol. The deafening sound of metal tearing. The silence of his dead, expectant wife. Sorrow. Loneliness. Desolation. That was six months ago and each day since had been a slow descent of self-inflicted misery, each day falling deeper into melancholy. He had chosen his path. He should be free of the suffering.

But why then this pain? Exquisite to the point it overpowered the senses, blotted out memories and clouded thought. Sam Saweel could do nothing but experience the pain. It emanated from the top of his head shooting through his neck, grinding his torso. Not a throbbing pain, but a constant, crushing pain. Pain such that it was the all of his existence.

Fighting to make sense of his predicament, Sam struggled to tear away his suffocating cocoon of agony. He had no sense of movement, no sense of orientation, size or shape. It was as if he were frozen in ice at the bottom of a huge glacier, immeasurable pressure assailing him from all sides, the deep cold oozing into his bones, congealing his blood, freezing the air in his lungs.

Pain distorts time. The greater its extent, the greater the distortion. It interdicts the time continuum, trapping its victim in a ceaseless loop of now. Sam's pain could have been going on for a lifetime or a millisecond.

He believed his eyes were open because his brain registered light. The pain prevented him from concentrating long enough to form a cohesive thought. He mustered his will to focus,

---

[2] "Instantaneous" appeared on line in *Busting and Droning Magazine*, 4/22/2014.

and the light would begin to coalesce into shapes only to be dispersed once again by pain's intrusion.

This tug-of-war between pain and perception wavered back and forth until Sam could force, by shear will, the images in the light to take form. Crimson blobs, like a red rain, appeared, suspended in his field of vision. Still the clash of pain and perception raged on. Slowly, other images took form.

Despite the inexorable pain, Sam held and studied these images. Struggling through timeless torment, he began to discern familiar patterns. The textures and shapes resembled the street in front of his office; but the images appeared upside down as if looking through a pinhole camera.

Why these images? Why now? Why this pain? This should not be! Pain obliterated the images once again. His psyche reeled with anguish. Constant torture racked his body. There was no rest, no acquittal of the onslaught of pain and confusion. Why?

He had chosen his path. Climb to the roof top. Jump. It was that simple. By his reckoning, three seconds of free fall, then instantaneous death followed by peaceful nothingness. The perfect remedy for a shattered existence. The perfect ending to a tragic play. Abandoning friends, family and God, he had finally set upon a course of action. No pain, no memories, no nothing. He would finally be free.

So he had thought.

DO YOU REMEMBER HOW TO FLY?

"Do you remember how to fly?" was how Froug started the conversation. His question caught me off guard. I had been working as a weekend orderly at Wrighthaven Hospital for barely two months. College was costly and I needed the money. Besides, I figured working in a hospital setting, even if it was a psychiatric facility, would provide a beneficial experience for a pre-med student. Wrighthaven was an old facility with a grimy, limestone façade that gave it the appearance of a prison. The gray clouds of January made it look all the more foreboding. Froug was always in the solarium, sitting in his worn wheelchair facing a window that overlooked the vast grounds surrounding the hospital. The sour smell of lunch trays waiting to be retrieved from the hallway spilled into the room. That was the only place I had ever encountered him. Until that point, I had never heard him say anything; I had not even seen him move. He was always attired in ubiquitous institutional clothing, faded blue robe struggling to cover striped pajamas, his bare feet shoved into dingy, terrycloth slippers. He had turned his head in my direction, clear, bright eyes focused directly on me.

"Oh, I never learned," I replied.

"I didn't ask you if you learned how to fly," he clipped back. "I asked if you remembered how to fly."

"Well, I've been on a plane a few times if that's what you mean."

"I don't care if you have been on an airplane, hot air balloon or rocket ship!" The frustration in his voice was palpable. "The question is very simple. Do you remember how to fly?"

"I guess I don't, then. Is there anything you need, anything I can help you with?" I asked.

"You probably can't remember talking with animals either, I bet."

"Oh, I talked to my dog all the time - when I was a kid."

He rolled his eyes. "You don't listen, do you? I asked if you remembered talking with animals - not *to* animals. There's a big difference you know. One is a conversation, the other is just making sounds."

"Well, excuse me for not making the fine distinctions," I shot back, immediately regretting the sarcasm in my voice. Wrighthaven was in the business of providing psychiatric services. Everyone on staff, including orderlies, was expected to be caring and positive in dealing with the residents. Unusual conversations were to be expected. This exchange was benign compared to some. "I'm sorry, didn't mean that the way it sounded. What was it you wanted to know?"

He had turned back to the window, seemingly oblivious to my apology.

* * *

For the next three weekend shifts, nothing transpired between us, not that I took any measures to speak with him during that time. I saw him in the solarium and checked on him as I did with the other residents. He never gave any acknowledgement of my presence.

On the fourth shift, as soon as I approached, he looked at me and picked up where he had left off a month earlier. "I wanted to know if you remembered how to fly and if you do, then it is obvious that you would remember talking with animals."

"Mr. Froug, can't say as I do."

"Call me Lazlo. No need to clutter one's mind with a second name," he continued. "I was like that. Couldn't remember, until I met Yardang. Asked me the same question. 'Do you remember how to fly?' I gave him a response much like you gave me."

"Oh, so you don't remember how to fly?"

"I said I couldn't remember until I met Yardang," Froug corrected. "It has taken many years, but I do remember now."

"How many years?" I asked.

"That's not important. Useless data. I didn't bother to count them so I wouldn't have to forget them," he replied.

"What was it like?" I asked, humoring him.

"Wonderful," he whispered. The face, usually void of expression, now beamed with joy.

I decided it was no harm to continue a conversation, no matter how outlandish, that obviously brought Froug so much enjoyment. Can a true smile be harmful?

"How does one learn to fly?" I asked.

Froug chortled. "Do you have to learn to breathe? Do you have to learn to roll over in bed? No! How does an infant learn to laugh? It doesn't - it sees an image, hears a sound, feels a sensation and voilà – you have laughter. It's there inside, innate, no lessons required. Much the same with flying. Though it is not really flying like a bird flapping its wings. Yardang characterized it as self-actuated instantaneous levitation. As good a description as any. Like riding a bicycle. You don't have to think about balance, it's just there. When you fly, you just move to where you want to be – except you don't use your feet. It's that simple."

"Sounds neat," I said, not wanting to challenge him. I had always heard that people with delusional thoughts construct elaborate explanations to support their claims. "So you just go. Must be great to zoom all over the place."

"It's not quite that easy," Froug said seriously. "You've been watching too many movies with caped superheroes if you believe you can just zoom all over the place. On the contrary, takes some thought and one must be careful. Just bash into a tree while not paying attention and see how good that feels."

"Well, I didn't mean it that way," I said, in hopes I hadn't offended him. He had seemed so happy and normal up to that point. But, I was too late. He had turned back to the window.

* * *

Just as before, nothing transpired between us for the next several weeks. Each time I saw him in the solarium, I tried to strike up a conversation. Each time, he ignored me, staring out the window as if I didn't exist. Then one afternoon, as soon as I approached, he looked at me, picking up where he had left as if nothing had happened.

"You see you've got to take it slow. Flying is not like walking around your backyard. Despite what you may have seen in the movies, Newton's laws of motion still apply. So zooming about might result in a nasty collision with a telephone pole. And you can't go up into the clouds, you'll freeze your butt off up there, not to mention there's not enough oxygen to keep you conscious."

"I never thought about that," I stammered.

"Of course you didn't. That's what you have to learn when it comes to flying, hopefully not the hard way. As for me, I just enjoyed gliding above the fields ever so slowly. Not even fast enough to stir the wildflowers. If you are very quiet, you can watch the field mice forage, smell the wild strawberries, or drift alongside a bee while it gathers nectar."

"Gosh, how could you ever forget something like that in the first place?" I asked. As soon as it jumped out of my mouth, I hoped he wouldn't take it wrong and clam-up again.

"Yardang explained it like this: each of us is born with these wonderful abilities, one of which is to fly, but they diminish over time as our brain is crammed full of useless information. We call it memory. Like a computer, once our brain's capacity is filled up, it can't do anything until some space is cleared.

"He went on to explain that the accumulation of memories is a terrible burden. Consider the insignificant pebble created at the birth of the universe, lollygagging through the void. Over the millennia, it collects bits of dust and debris, the detritus of the Big Bang. The more it collects, the more it attracts, growing in size like a snowball rolling down the hillside. It floats along through the cosmos, snatching up all that it encounters until the original pebble, trapped at the core is crushed beyond recognition under the weight of all that surrounds it. Its essence, what it was is no longer recognizable, diluted in the conglomerate. In like manner, our mind is crushed under the weight of memories. Those primal abilities we were born with are similarly diluted in the cacophony of memories that fill our minds and ultimately pushed into the dark and lonely corners of our psyche."

By that point, his voice had increased in speed and enthusiasm. I found his arguments fascinating and even though I was sure they were flights of fancy, I wanted to hear more. He must have sensed some doubt on my part because he suddenly fell silent. For an instant, I thought the spell had been broken and he would once again turn toward the window. Instead, he continued to look me right in the eye. He waited long enough for my anxiety to build before he drew in a measured breath and began to speak.

"You have doubts. Consider the plight of a Russian man, many years ago, who had the ability to recall everything he had seen or heard. The famed neuropsychologist, Luria, studied him for 20 years. He asked the man to memorize all manner of things ranging from long sequences of random numbers to poems in foreign languages, all of which he did with apparent ease. His ability was so strong he could retain them all and recall them years, even decades later. The man eventually went on to perform as a mnemonic. However, in time, the accumulation of memories created great confusion in his mind. So much so, he quit to spend the rest of his life attempting to forget them. It is said he finally found peace when he learned to consciously identify and remove them one by one from his mind. A conscious unremembering so to speak. This really happened, you can check the facts.

"Which brings the discussion full circle. You see I was determined to remove the unnecessary from my mind so that I could once again remember how to fly. I will not remove everything. I wish to remember my Mother's face. But for the most part, my mind, which was incapacitated with worthless information, is now clear. I remember only the good stuff."

"So you remember how to fly?" I asked.

"Of course."

"Why don't you?"

"How do you know I haven't?" he answered with a question.

"You got me there, I only work on the weekends. I guess you have all the weekdays to fly about."

A wry smile puckered up on his lips. "There was one thing Yardang asked me to do before I decided to fly again."

"And what's that?" I asked.

Too late, he had turned back to the window.

* * *

The last time I saw Froug, his wheel chair had been rolled out on the porch attached to the solarium. It was a bright, balmy April day. I stepped out from the cool shadows into the warm sunlight. I could see a squirrel sitting on its haunches next to Froug. It scampered off as I approached.

Without turning his head, Froug said, "Yardang said I had to pass it along."

"About flying?"

"Yes, about flying." Froug took a deep breath. "Doesn't that air smell wonderful?" he whispered. "I was just having a conversation with that squirrel before you came up."

"I hope I didn't scare him off," I said.

"No, we were done." Froug waived his arm off to the left. "He said there is a lovely field beyond those hills. The wild flowers are just popping out. I think I'll go take a look. Remember, you must pass it on."

* * *

As much as I tried to explain, the hospital administrators and the police just would not believe that Froug flew away. That was many years ago. I don't count them, so I won't have to forget them. I've been here at Wrighthaven Hospital ever since, although not on the payroll. I don't mind. After all, Yardang said the accumulation of memories is a terrible burden, and the solarium is as good a place to unremember as any.

I've got a new shrink. Nice young lady right out of school. We've had a couple of conversations. It won't be long now, Spring is just around the corner and a squirrel said "Hi" to me the other day.

45

A WALK IN THE PARK

A flawless sky stretched above Ian in all directions. Not the piercing sapphire hue of a mid-western summer day as expected; rather, a soft, robin's egg tint filled the vast, overhead expanse. Its chroma was probably due to the higher oxygen content of this ancient atmosphere. *Blue, is not a popular color in this environment.* The wide cerulean mirror of lake below and the sky above were all to suggest that this pigment existed at all. *Does nature have something against the royal hue, or is it simply an oversight?*

Green was a different story. *This must be nature's favorite child, doted on and lavished with unfettered affection and attention.* Every imaginable gradation of color burst forth to tantalize the eye. Lush tints flooded the landscape. Vast stands of giant viridian seed ferns filled the forest; forming the forest's jagged canopy. Smaller ferns cloaked in spring's fresh verdure formed the undergrowth. All the same, all different, iridescent against the dark loam of the forest floor. Between, robust emerald conifers dotted the landscape.

He walked through the prehistoric landscape, his senses feasting. It stood in stark contrast to the sterile cocoon which formed his day to day existence. The aroma of life filled his head. He knelt down, his knee sinking in the soft black soil, to examine an emerging fern. Its soft fiddlehead was unfurling. *It hasn't changed for millions of years.* He was struck with an overwhelming urge to pluck the crosier. Trembling fingers reached out and gently grasped the shoot, which snapped off without resistance. It was cool to the touch. Pulling it close to his face, he inhaled its earthy fragrance . He had not smelled anything so fresh and vibrant for a very long time. His was a world of recycled odors. Nothing fresh, nothing alive. His universe was a soggy amalgam of leftover breath and the oily flavor of a manufactured environment. Even the scents produced to mask the dulling odor of confined life smothered everything in a cloying artificial sweetness, a constant reminder of a bleak existence devoid of nature's cleansing breath.

He took the fiddlehead in his mouth with the reverence a priest would use to place a host on a child's tongue. A glorious flavor filled his mouth. He was reminded of the fresh sugar snap peas his grandmother would pick from the vine and serve in her big blue bowl. No cooking there. Crunchy and sweet, they needed no processing; didn't need to be macerated into the mush now shamelessly called food. Savoring the gentle resistance of the fresh pulp to his teeth and tongue, he chewed slowly, experiencing the textures against his palate and cheeks. He reached for another and hesitated: an act of reverence.

As the aroma of the fern cleared, he became aware of the strong odor of the soil. The smells of the forest were layered. As he walked among the conifers, the pungent odor of pine filled his head. It reminded him of boyhood days spent playing the pine woods of Georgia where his cousins lived. He stooped down, The verdant bouquet of the ferns filled his head with the crisp odor of chlorophyll and oxygen. It smelled of life. It smelled like his mother's garden in the back yard of his youth. There were no plants, no living things where he lived now. Sometimes, he thought even he was not a living thing; rather just another gadget among the countless gadgets packed away in neat little compartments waiting to be taken out and activated.

He dug his fingers into the damp earth and hefted a heaping mound of the rich black soil. It was cool and damp and weighed heavily in his hand. The decaying vegetation and bacteria combined to produce a dark odor - a brown odor. It filled his head and confronted his olfactory nerves in stark contrast to the delicate aroma of the fiddlehead fern. *Brown, is another of nature's favored colors. Definitely not as dear as green, but still, nature uses it abundantly.* He slowly sifted the contents of his hand, enjoying the soft friction on his skin as it splayed through his fingers, floating back down to the forest floor. He stared intently as the material drained away. He could see the tiny bits of decaying vegetation and the tiny insects who, oblivious to his presence or their sudden relocation, remained busily at work breaking down these bits of fern and pine cone to provide the next generation's breakfast. After the soil had drained away, he hefted another fist-full, bringing it up to his nose to inhale another draft of its thick aroma, and then stared at the disappearing earth as intently as he had the first time.

The first shock wave arrived simultaneously with an earsplitting explosion, knocking him to the ground. The force of the blast made the forest floor, which had felt so soft when he had knelt down, now feel as hard as the composite deck of the ship. Dust and debris filled the air and he choked down a gulp of acrid air, struggling to regain his footing. Ahead, a fissure opened up. The seed ferns and conifers pushed aside , falling to the forest floor, bursting into flame like matchsticks. Billowing black smoke shot up through the gaping maw of raw soil and rock. Another explosion blasted out, hammering the air from his lungs. Waves of heat slapped his face as he watched molten rock spew from the forest floor. Razor sharp fern leaves slashed at his arms, and stinging beads of crimson blood welled up through every cut. The metallic taste of blood filled his throat mingling with the bitter bile that oozed up from his stomach. Sulphurous smoke clogged his lungs, making each breath an agonizing effort. He ran wildly, feeling the heat growing on his back. He looked over his shoulder. The earth belched an angry orange river of molten rock, spewing over the opening, rising like a tsunami, bearing down on him with incredible speed.

The lake lay just ahead. If he could make the water, he might have a chance. He looked once again over his shoulder to gauge his chances. Turning back, his right leg shot calf-deep into a jumble of roots. The sound of his leg shattering reached his ears at the same moment the exquisite pain of a compound fracture reached his brain. Screaming in agony and fear, he looked down to see the jagged tips of his severed tibia and fibula rip through his flesh, blood spewing from the gaping wound. Behind him, viscous lava pounded to the ground like a wave on the breakers. A slow surge of sullen heat crept forward. Every movement brought excruciating pain. Blisters formed on his arms and then erupted as the serum reached the boiling point. His clothes smoldered. The stench of his own burning flesh filled his nose. He gasped for air just as the forest around him burst into flame.

* * *

Migo checked the readout twice before calling out to Herve. "Hey, take a look at the readout for Arus, I. C."

"What's up?"

"Readout says we got an off liner. Jump Stasis Unit 137."

Herve quickly swept his hand over the glowing touch screen until the readout for JSU137 appeared. "Crap, I hate off liners. Let's go, it's on level 5."

Migo and Herve made their way down the tight corridors to the pneumolift, descended to level 5 and then to the jump stasis unit numbered 137. Migo tapped his access code on the screen. The readout blinked on.

"Same indication here. Let's open it up," he said, entering the command to activate the animation sequence in the event a readout malfunction had occurred and the occupant was still on line. A blast of stale air confronted the two as the door to the unit slid open. Herve reached in to feel for a pulse on the occupant while Migo scanned the readout data.

"Looks like the readout was right," said Migo.

"Stupid, it's always right. Any idea on what happened?"

Migo called up the data. "Interesting, all vitals within normal parameters until the last few minutes, then everything falls off the chart.

"Everything?"

"Yeah man. This is interesting. Right before he off lined, there was a huge spike in adrenaline, followed by a massive calcium dump. That would account for everything going haywire. With that much go juice released into the blood stream, your heart would knot up like a fist."

"So what happens then?

"A sudden drop in blood pressure, loss consciousness, then you die, idiot, just like our friend here."

"What would cause that to happen?"

"I don't know, let the med techs make that call. Get the number off the senchip so we can note it in the report."

"OK." Herve gently removed the senpod from the cadaver's head. He pulled the senchip and scanned it. "Hey, this ain't company issue. Looks like it's got a whole different configuration than I ever seen."

"Get all the particulars for the report," said Migo.

"Guess he didn't want to ride out his jump listening to delta binaural waves and watching snow fall with a company issued chip."

"Can you blame him?" asked Migo. "I know you got to use a senpod to maintain minimal brain wave activity while you're in stasis, but those company programs suck."

"Says here the title is 'Triassic Journeys'. Probably bought it from a street vendor at the last port of call."

"Well that's how I want to go out," Mingo laughed, "dreaming a peaceful walk through the Triassic park."

THE PROTECTOR[3]

Luda stood peering into the deep shadows. The bright flowers and lush field grass in which she stood stopped abruptly at the base of the tall oak trees. Their thick and twisted trunks supported a canopy of leaves blocking all sunlight from the forest floor. Behind her, Maks and Anya played quietly along the creek that meandered across the meadow.

"Make sure Maks and Anya are safe." mother had said as Luda stepped from the cottage porch. It was a task she took seriously.

She knew the beast was there. Babushka had told her of Zicgaforja lurking deep in the shadows of the forest. Even the village woodcutter with his broad, double bladed axe for protection avoided this forest. Behind the trees in the darkness, long dead leaves rustled on the forest floor. *Is that the faint, dark scent of the creature floating on the wood's cold, damp breath?* It chased away the fragile warmth of the Spring sun, sending a chill through her. Regardless, she stood her ground, eyes never turning away.

While the children played blissfully, Luda stood between them and the waiting evil. She held her staff at the ready by her side. The beast was patient, waiting for its prey to come within range – muscles tensed, poised to attack with ripping teeth and tearing claws.

Mother's call came rolling over the meadow, breaking her concentration. Maks and Anya jumped up from their play, setting off toward home. Luda turned with one last intent stare into the dark recesses of the woods and called out in smug defiance,

[3] "The Protector" appeared on line in *StrippedLit500 Fiction Magazine*, Issue 3 – 3/2017.

"Lucky for you Zicgaforja, Mama has called us for supper." With that, she threw the twig she had been holding into the shadows and turned to join her brother and sister in a race back to the cottage.

WHIRLIGIG MAN

"That will conclude our lesson on wind power as a source of renewable energy,' said Ms. Morgan. "Remember, you have a quiz on Friday, so everyone should review their lessons. Now, before we go to lunch, I have a special treat for you. We have studied wind power, and now it is time to see some in action. I have asked a special guest to visit with us this morning. He has a very interesting hobby. If everyone will follow me, we will walk single file out to the parking lot."

Joshua slapped his book shut and shoved it under his seat. Falling in at the end of the line, he followed Ms. Morgan and his classmates out into the parking lot. The sun shone down from the crisp blue sky, very pleasant for an early spring day. Breezes gusted under puffy clouds.

An old pickup truck was parked at the end of the pavement. A man rummaged around in the back of the truck. He retrieved a long pole. Looking up at the sky, he stuck a finger in his mouth then held it up above his head. Joshua could swear the man looked straight at him before stuck it in the ground with three other poles.

"A perfect day for whirligigs," the man sang out as they approached. He was rangy, dressed in a flannel shirt and khakis. A shock of silver hair perched over his tanned, smiling face. The children stood a respectful distance from the man.

"Come on, come on, don't be shy," he said. He stood next to the four poles, each topped with a thin metal rod. "No one ever learned anything by hanging back. Besides, this won't be on the quiz, will it Ms. Morgan?"

"Of course not," she said. While the rest of the children inched closer, Joshua hung back. "Class, let me introduce Mr. Michael Engel. I met him at October Fest where I found out he has the most fascinating hobby. He makes whirligigs. I thought it would be perfect for our section on wind power. That's why I asked him here today. Does anyone know what a whirligig is?" She looked for a hand, but none were to be found. "Well, never mind, Mr. Engel will tell us about whirligigs and how they relate to wind power. Mr. Engel, they're all yours."

"Thanks Ms. Morgan. My full name is Michael Archibald Engel, which is quite a mouthful, even for me. So why don't you call me Mr. Arch and we'll all get along just fine. A whirligig is a very simple thing. It has at least one part that spins or whirls in the wind. Whirligigs are also called pinwheels, buzzers, gee-haws, spinners, or just whirlys. They've been around since medieval times. They probably came to America with the settlers from England, so you can see they have been part of our culture from the start."

Joshua was already bored.

"With few exceptions," Arch continued, "whirligigs don't have any purpose but to entertain us. They are very small, most of them can be held in your hand. Most of the early ones consisted of a carved figure whose arms were free to spin in the wind. It could be a soldier with a sword in each hand valiantly fighting the wind or a farmer with an axe in each hand furiously chopping wood. Later, whirligigs got more complicated, but they were almost always fanciful. But you don't want to hear me talk all day, I bet you'd rather see some gigs in action wouldn't you?"

"Yes," rang out the reply.

Joshua rolled his eyes.

"OK, you wait here while I get some." Arch looked at the children. He focused in on a thin boy with curly brown hair and hazel eyes standing at the back. "I might need some help. Since you're closest to the truck, how about it?"

"That's Joshua," said Ms. Morgan. "He'll be happy to help."

"Follow me," said Arch. When they reached the tailgate, he said, "Here you go," lifting a wooden figure from the truck bed.

Joshua held out his hands to receive the brightly decorated figure of a baseball player with a bat in each hand. Joshua move one of the arms. As it swept up, the arm on the other side moved down. Something interesting for a change he thought. The bats, were wide and flat and tilted like a fan blade.

"He's one of my favorites," Arch said retrieving another figure. It was a bird with scalloped wings on either side. Unlike the baseball player, this figure had double wings which resembled propellers mounted on either side. "Let's go set these up and we'll come back for the others in a minute."

By the time they got back, the class had started to fidget. "Looks like we're just in time," Arch laughed, "Let me have the one with the baseball uniform," he said. Joshua handed over the figure. "This is 'Casey'," Arch said, holding up the figure. "Named him after the poem 'Casey At The Bat'. Maybe Ms. Morgan will read it to you later. We'll put him up and when a breeze comes along, you'll see what he does," he said placing 'Casey' on the pole. "When the breeze hits his arms, they spin." The sun popped out from behind a cloud shining brightly on the baseball player. A gust of wind picked up, sending Casey's arms spinning furiously, sunlight glinting off the whirling bats. The class oohed and aahed.

"What else have you got there?" he said turning to Joshua. "It's a bird."

"This is a red-winged blackbird, the herald of Spring," said Arch. "When he flies, warm weather is just around the corner."

"Mr. Engel, I thought the first robin was the sign of Spring," Ms. Morgan said.

"A common myth, like our famous cousin, Punxsutawney Phil, that pampered Pennsylvania groundhog, revered as a predictor of weather. Lots of fun to talk about, but if you really want to know when Spring has arrived, look for the red-winged black bird. I'll venture to predict that if our friend here flies today, Spring will come tomorrow."

"Well, Mr. Engel, that's a pretty bold prediction," said Ms. Morgan. "I think we have a considerable bit of Winter left before warm weather is here to stay. In fact, I think snow flurries are predicted for the rest of the week."

"There's only one way to find out," Arch said, dropping the bird in place. The breeze picked up as the clouds cleared. The sun beamed down and the figure's wings began to spin. Joshua helped bring out two more whirligigs, which they set on the poles. The wind kept up a steady flow under the bright sun and the children were quite warm by lunch time.

"Can Mr. Arch eat lunch with us?" Joshua asked.

"Why certainly," Ms. Morgan said. "Would you care to join us for lunch, Mr. Engel? I think we are having mystery meat burgers again today."

"Wouldn't miss it for the world. Been lots of places and eaten everything from sasqu to haggis. I'm sure this will be quite tasty compared to some of the food I've eaten."

Joshua helped Arch through the lunch line and they chose a table close to the windows to keep an eye on the whirligigs, which were spinning happily in the breeze. After a few minutes of silence, Joshua asked, "What's sasqu?"

"A form of ancient gruel. It's like soupy oatmeal."

"Yuk."

"Don't knock it till you try it, although I doubt you'll find any around here. As for what haggis is made of, you don't even want to ask. But enough of all that. What'd you think of the whirligigs?"

"They're Okay."

"Just Okay?"

"No, well, I guess they're pretty cool. Did you make them?"

"Sure did."

"Dad used to make neat stuff like that. He had a workshop and everything with all kinds of tools and stuff. Whenever anyone needed something fixed, they brought it to Dad."

"I'd like to meet him sometime."

Joshua hung his head and stared at his half eaten lunch. After a moment of silence, he said, "Dad's a soldier. Been MIA since last summer."

"Well, Joshua, I'm sorry to hear that," said Arch. "Sounds like he's a good guy."

"Me and him used to build a lot of stuff together. He built me a tool box and gave me some of his tools to put in it."

"That's nice, keep that tool box so you two can make things again when he comes home. I'd like to see his workshop some time."

"Mom had to sell some of his stuff to pay the bills." Joshua paused for a moment then stood up. "I'm done, can we go back out?"

"Sure."

Outside, they joined some students and teachers who had gathered around the display. Arch answered their questions while the whirligigs spun in the breeze. When the bell rang, the children began to filter back to their classrooms. Joshua lingered by the truck.

"Better get inside, before you get a tardy, Joshua," Arch warned as he lifted one of the larger whirligigs from its post. "I wouldn't want Ms. Morgan to get after me for enticing you to stay out here after the bell."

"Do you need any help?" Joshua asked.

"Not now, but if you've a mind to, I've some projects at home that could use the assistance of a bright young man like yourself. You interested?"

"I guess so."

"Alright then, write your phone number on this." Arch pulled a notebook from his pocket. "I'll call your mother and square it with her. Now git before the late bell rings."

"OK," Joshua said as he scribbled the phone number on the pad. Then he trotted off toward the entrance. He stopped about midway and turned his head. "Thanks, Mr. Arch."

"You're welcome."

After two days without a call, Joshua started to think Mr. Arch had forgotten all about the invitation. As he left school, he stopped at the bike rack to peel off his sweatshirt. Unusually warm winds had pushed the cold far to the north. He hopped up on his bike and started for home. Along the way, he tried not to think about whirligigs and broken promises.

After a few minutes, he was home. He coasted up the driveway, parking his bike by the back steps. A flutter of motion caught his eye. A red-wing blackbird had landed on the bird feeder and was pecking at a seed. It peered at Joshua with one eye then the other.

After pouring a large glass of milk, he changed from his school clothes and went outside to enjoy the rest of the warm afternoon. His mother would not be home for a while, so he rode his bike down the street to look for some adventure. When he returned, he saw her car parked behind the house. He propped his bike against the house then ran up the steps.

"Mom, guess what I saw today?" he called out, busting into the kitchen.

"Joshie, how many times have I asked you not to slam the door?" she said wiping her hands on thread bare, faded jeans, at least 10 years out of style. "How about a hug?"

"Sorry Mom, but I saw a red-winged black bird. Mr. Arch said they are a sure sign Spring is here," Joshua said, stepping into his mother's outstretched arms. He had shot up over the winter and now was almost as tall as her. He had her curly hair, but without the gray that betrayed her age.

"Is this Mr. Arch's last name Engle?" she asked.

"Yeah, that's him"

"He called today to ask if you could go over to his house to see his whirli-things."

"Whirligigs," Joshua corrected.

"Whirli-things, whirligigs, no matter. He tried to explain what they were, but I couldn't make heads or tails of what he was talking about. Are they some kind of action figure?"

"No, Mom. They're kinda cool. Maybe I'll make one and we can put it up in the yard. You'd like 'em."

"Well, I'm sure I'll like it whatever it is. He said he was at your school."

"Yeah, Ms. Morgan had him show us his whirligigs."

"That's what he said. Well, I guess if Ms. Morgan trusts him, it's Okay. He doesn't live very far from here. Out on Legion Pike. You can ride your bike over there Saturday after you pick up you room. I'll call him tomorrow and let him know it's Okay."

"Thanks, Mom," he said, "and please don't call me Joshie."

The next day at school crept along so slowly that Joshua thought the clock was running backwards. If it had not been for the fact that it was Friday, he would have gone crazy waiting for the weekend. As it was, most of his day was spent looking out the school window picturing the whirligigs spinning round. That evening, he made sure to pick up his room so he could get an early start the next day.

In the morning, Joshua wolfed down the oatmeal his mother had fixed. He thought about sasqu and wondered if it was as unappealing as the concoction in his bowl. He drained his milk in one long gulp, then quickly rinsed his dishes and stacked them haphazardly in the dishwasher.

"Can I go now?" he asked.

"Is your room picked up?"

"Yes."

"OK then. Mind that you do what Mr. Engel says, and be home before supper."

"Sure thing Mom," he called out, shooting through the door. He took off down the drive with a running start, jumping on his bike. At the end of the street, he came to a skidding stop. He dropped his bike and ran back to his house. He shot through the door and bounded up the steps to his room. Flinging open the door to his closet, he dropped to his knees, digging through the mound of clothes, shoes and toys in the corner. Tucked away in the very back of the closet, he found what he was searching for.

"What's the matter Joshie?" his mother asked.

"Almost forgot it."

"Forgot what?"

"My tool box." Joshua looked at the scattered contents of the closet which now spread out into the room. He nudged it all back inside with his foot and turned to his mother. "Can I straighten it up when I get back?" She stood squarely in the doorway, arms folded. He knew he was at her mercy.

She stepped forward and held out her arms. "I thought you were going to leave without giving me a hug." Joshua put his arms around her. She kissed him on the forehead and said "Be careful and have fun."

The ride to Arch's house route took him past row after row of aging starter homes, their once bright paint now faded and peeling. Eventually, the sidewalks along the tightly packed streets melted away. Soon he was on crumbling blacktop, passing much older, frame houses situated on large overgrown lots. He knew he had reached his destination when he spied a large whirligig planted on a whitewashed fence post. He saw Arch sitting on the porch.

"Right on time," he said, checking an imaginary watch on his wrist. "Had any sasqu lately?"

"Mom made oatmeal for breakfast," Joshua panted.

"Close enough. Let's visit awhile before we get started."

They sat on the porch the better part of an hour getting acquainted. Joshua was anxious to get going on whatever it was they were going to do, not realizing, in Arch's way of thinking, talking was part of the agenda. Soon enough though, he got up from his rocker and said,

"Well enough of this chit-chat, what say you and I head around to the shop and see what mischief we can get into." Joshua jumped up. grabbing his tool box. "It's that-a-way," Arch said jabbing his thumb over his shoulder like he was hitching a ride.

"How about I follow you?" Joshua asked.

"Come on, then," Arch said, disappearing around the corner of the porch. Joshua followed him along a well worn path to a small frame building. It sported a fresh coat of white paint. The trim was painted green with gold accents. As they approached, Joshua could read the hand painted sign that hung over the door.

The Wonder Whirligig Works
If It Works, It's A Wonder!
Arch Engel, Prop.

"What kind of whirligig is that?" Joshua asked, pointing to a spinning object mounted on a slender pole half way to the workshop. It had four arms attached to an ornate central hub. Brass cups, lying on their sides, were attached to each arm.

"Oh, that's not really a whirligig: It's an anemometer. It measures wind speed. They use 'em in weather stations. The wind causes the cups to spin. You can judge wind speed by how fast this thing spins around."

"D'you make it?" Joshua asked.

"No, no, it was made by Dr. John Robinson, of the Armagh Observatory, over a hundred years ago." Arch explained while Joshua watched the cups whirl around in the morning breeze. "Bet your dad would like this," Arch added.

"Yeah," whispered Joshua.

They went inside the workshop. Whirligigs occupied every available space not devoted to tools and works in progress. Some were simple like 'Casey'. Others had many moving parts. The shop was neatly organized. Joshua immediately felt comfortable in its cozy surroundings. For the remainder of the morning, he listened as Arch explained each contraption.

"Well, before we get going on a project, I think some lunch would be in order. You hungry?" asked Arch

"Sure."

"Let's head back to the house. I'll fix some sandwiches." Arch led the way. Inside was a large country style kitchen. A wooden table filled the center of the room.

"Put some plates on the table," Arch said while he sliced some bread from a large brown loaf. "Hope you don't mind some homemade bread. I like it a lot better than the stuff you get at the grocery nowadays. You'll find the plates in that cupboard," he added, pointing back over his shoulder with the big knife he was using to slice the bread. "Should be some glasses there too."

Joshua laid the plates and set a tumbler next to each. "What about knives and forks?" he asked.

"In the drawer by the oven. There's lemonade and milk in the fridge. I'll take some lemonade, you can pour yourself what you like."

In a few minutes, they were sitting at the table ready to eat. "I always say a prayer before my meal, how about you?"

"Sure."

After they finished, Arch said, "Well dig in, hope you like ham and cheese."

"Anything is OK as long as it isn't mystery meat," Joshua laughed.

"Or haggis," added Arch.

After lunch they returned to the workshop. They spent the rest of the afternoon fashioning a new whirligig. They had finished all the rough cuts and had started sanding when Arch said, "Well, time has certainly flown by. I'm afraid it's time for you to be heading home. How about we put this one up until you can come back?"

"Do I have 'ta go now?"

"We wouldn't want to disappoint your mom first time out would we?"

"No, I guess not."

"Come back in time for breakfast next Saturday, and we'll work on it all day. Okay?"

"Okay."

Arch showed Joshua how put all the tools in their proper places. On the ride home, Joshua pictured what the finished whirligig would look like and how fast it would spin in the breeze. The trip, which had seemed to take an eternity in the morning, sped by. Soon he was wheeling up his own driveway. He looked for the red winged blackbird, but did not see any sign of him. He walked into the kitchen, careful not to let the door slam. His mother was peeling potatoes at the sink.

She glanced up at the clock above the stove. "Back in time for supper, I see. How'd your day go?"

"Okay."

"Just Okay?"

"Well, I meant it went real good. We worked on a new whirligig. We're going to paint it next Saturday. That's if I can go back. Mr. Arch said it was OK. I can go, can't I?"

"If you do your chores and all your homework, I guess you can. What do you think of Mr. Engle?"

"He's a lot like Dad, but not exactly."

"Is that a good thing?"

"Oh yeah."

The week passed slowly for Joshua. He made sure to do his chores and all his homework assignments. He got up at first daylight on Saturday and packed his tool kit and the cookies his mother had made as a thank you. This time the trip to Arch's house did not seem to take as long as it had the first time. The temperature had remained warm and buds were pushing out from dormant branches. Flocks of robins filled the sky.

After a couple of Saturdays, Joshua brought home the new whirligig. He convinced his mother to let him put it in the back yard where she could see it from the kitchen window. As Joshua's skills developed, he and Arch planned more elaborate whirligigs. The two spent almost every Saturday working in Arch's workshop. Joshua's mother even invited Arch over for Sunday dinner. He brought fresh baked bread and a curried fruit dish that went very well with the roast chicken she had prepared. Afterward, they all sat in the back yard and talked while watching the whirligig spin.

One Saturday, on his way home, Joshua was surprised to see a whirligig had been placed in the yard of what he thought had been a vacant house. It was not at all like the whirligigs he was used to seeing at Arch's. This one was some kind of wild animal that raised up its forelegs as if it were going to leap off of its platform. Joshua stopped, to get a closer look. He studied every detail. Perhaps there was something he and Arch could use for one of their whirligigs.

"Ain't nice to steal other folks' whirligig ideas, " said a voice behind Joshua. His heart leapt. A man dressed in scruffy, ill fitting clothes stepped behind him. A grimy cabbie hat was pulled low on his forehead covering his eyes with a dark shadow. Several days growth of stubble pushed out from sallow cheeks.

"Oh, sorry, I wasn't trying to steal your ideas. I just like whirligigs," Joshua apologized.

"So's you say. Not many kids are interested in these things now a days. Too busy looking at what they shouldn't be looking at on the internet."

Joshua stared at the scruffy man not knowing what to think. "I guess I better be going, now."

"What's your hurry? I got a lot of these things around back. If you ain't here to steal any ideas like you says, why don't you check 'em out?"

"Well, it's getting late and I'm supposed to be getting home."

"Oh come on. Nobody cares one way or another about a few minutes. Tell your mommy you lost track of time. It's none of her business anyway. You're big enough to make some decisions on your own aren't you? Don't you want to see my workshop?"

"Well, I guess, but I really should get home."

"Whatever suits ya kid," the scruffy man said turning away.

Joshua got back on his bike and pedaled with all his might, thinking of the whirligig and the man he had just met. All through the week, his thoughts kept drifting back to his encounter. When Saturday finally rolled around, Joshua rode as fast as he could until he saw the whirligig again. The wild animal was leaping up and down, up and down, driven by the morning breeze. Joshua slowed as he passed in front of the house, looking for any sign of its occupant. Seeing no one about, he kept on till he reached Arch's home.

He didn't say anything to Arch about the whirligig or the scruffy man. For some reason, Joshua was uncomfortable at the prospect of telling Arch what had happened. As the day wore on, he wondered what the other workshop was like and what kinds of whirligigs might be found there.

About mid-afternoon, he mustered up his courage and said to Arch, "I forgot to tell you that I have to leave early today. Got some things I have to do before supper." He felt uncomfortable. It was not a lie, but it was not the whole story either.

"Sure thing," Arch answered. His smile and easy agreement made Joshua feel even worse.

The ride seemed to take forever. Eventually, a whirligig came into view. When he was near enough to make out the details, he could see that a new whirligig was perched on the fence post. He hopped off his bike and moved in for a closer look. This whirligig was set up like a windmill. Between the blades and the rudder, a witch rocked to and fro on her broom.

The scruffy man appeared. "Still stealin' ideas, I see."

"I'm not stealing your ideas. Just wanted to see how this worked. It's pretty neat."

"Want to see some others, or have you got to run home to mommy?"

"I don't have to run anywhere," Joshua huffed. "I can stay as long as I like."

"Well, that's more like it," the scruffy man cackled, walking off in the direction of the house. Joshua followed, pushing his bike over the thick weeds that covered the yard. The scruffy man kept walking without saying a word or looking back, until he disappeared around the corner of the house. As Joshua trotted along, he glanced through the dirty windows. He could not see any curtains or blinds at the windows, the rooms appeared empty. Once he passed the corner of the house, a dilapidated shed came into view. A few remnants of peeling black paint remained around the warped window sills. Curling shingles almost void of their red grit coating clung to the sagging roof. The scruffy man took the key that hung from a chain around his neck and unlocked the padlock.

Joshua leaned his bike against the side of the building and followed the man as he stepped into the dark confines of the workshop. Inside, after his eyes adjusted to the dim light, Joshua was confronted by stacks of dust and cobweb covered whirligigs piled everywhere in the workshop. In contrast to Arch's shop, grubby, rusting tools and piles of materials lay haphazardly on a large table in the center of the room. Despite this, Joshua was fascinated by the place. The scruffy man motioned for him to sit on a stool. Then, he blew the dust off one whirligig after another showing each to Joshua. They were all dark and sinister in composition, quite unlike the whirligigs that Arch preferred.

Some time passed before Joshua looked at his watch and realized that he would have to hurry to get home before supper. "Thanks a lot for showing me all your stuff Mister. . . . " Joshua hesitated, realizing he did not know the scruffy man's name.

"Hobbs Hanbi," the man declared, peering into Joshua's eyes. "Call me Hobbs. Not Mr. Hanbi, not Mr. Hobbs, not Uncle, or even Your Honorable Honor. Just Hobbs. Got it?"

"Sure, whatever you say is Okay with me," Joshua stammered, quite surprised by Hobbs' sudden outburst.

"You should come back when we have more time to visit," Hobbs cooed. "I think you and I could have a bit of fun if we tried. Don't you?"

"Well, I don't know. . . "

"Don't know!" Hanbi interrupted. "Why a smart boy like you always knows what he wants. Come over this Wednesday, and I'll show you something real interesting."

"Oh, that's a school day, and it would be too late to come all this way after school."

"Who said anything about after school? Why not come for the whole day?"

"I couldn't miss school."

"Why not. I bet you spend most of the time looking out the window, don't you? What difference is one measly day going to make? You're a smart kid, one day don't mean anything. How many years you been going to school, never missing a day. Don't you deserve a day off? Nobody cares."

"But I can't just skip, Mom would be sore at me," Joshua pleaded.

"We can fix that. Just take a note in Tuesday, explaining that you have to go to a funeral out of town or something like that. It's easy. Let me show you," Hobbs soothed, grabbing a pad of note paper from the cluttered table. He pulled a pen from his pocket, hunching over the paper. Joshua watched his arm move with the pen strokes. "There you go," Hobbs sneered, handing the note to Joshua. "One note excusing you from school next Wednesday - urgent family business out of town." Joshua hesitantly took the note and examined it. He was amazed at how much it looked like his mother's handwriting.

Joshua tried to hand it back. "No, I couldn't," he said. "It just wouldn't be right."

"Wouldn't be right?" Hobbs spumed, holding his hand up refusing to take back the note. "I'll bet your teacher has missed a day or two, hasn't she?"

"Well that's different."

"What d'ya mean different? I'll bet she's taken off a day to go shopping or just lay around and watch TV. Everybody does it. Ain't it about time you caught on? Let me ask you. Do they flunk you if you miss a day? Do they make you stay after school? Naw. They expect you to miss some time. It don't hurt nobody. But, if you want to spend every day sitting there listening to the same old crap, it's no skin off my nose. Go ahead, if that's what you want to do." He shook his head in disbelief. Joshua held out the note. "Listen, kid, do me a favor. Hang on to that. Call it a souvenir if you like. There ain't no date on it, so's you could use it any time you like. If, all of a sudden, you decide you'd like to do something other than count the ceiling tiles in your classroom, you can always fill in the date. If not, c'est la vie. See ya 'round kid."

Joshua hesitated for a moment then folded the note and stuck it in his pocket. "Well, thanks for showing me your whirligigs and stuff. Maybe I'll stop again sometime."

"Yeah, yeah, kid," snorted Hobbs.

Joshua took that as his signal to hustle out the door. He pushed his bike as fast as he could over the clumpy weeds until he reached the road. He was relieved to feel the rush of air in his face as he set out for home.

He rushed through the kitchen door just as his mother was pulling a casserole from the oven. "You cut it close today," she said.

"I guess we lost track of time."

"Anything interesting happen today?"

"Naw, just the same old stuff."

"You're not getting tired of going to Mr. Engles's are you?"

"No, no, I didn't mean that. Everything's Okay."

"Alright, go wash up before your food gets cold. I fixed mac 'n cheese."

Although Joshua made his best effort to pay attention to supper, his thoughts were on his strange experience with Hobbs.

The strange little man and his dingy, cluttered workshop intrigued and attracted Joshua. He envied Hobbs, who seemed quite comfortable with thumbing his nose at authority and order when it suited him.

Joshua wandered what the harm would be in playing hooky for a day. The more he replayed Hobbs' words in his mind, the more appealing and seductive they became. The note, which Hobbs had so painstakingly written, itched in his pocket. After supper, Joshua slipped up to his room and stashed the note deep in his closet, hoping he would forget it was there.

The next Saturday, Joshua set out extra early for Arch's house. As he neared the spot where he had encountered Hobbs, he felt uneasy. He had tried to think of another route to take so he could avoid going past the place, but he couldn't find one. He hoped an early start might get him past before Hobbs was up and about. As for the ride home, he would deal with that when it happened. He breathed a sigh of relief as he saw there was no new whirligig on the fencepost. Pedaling for all he was worth, Joshua sped past the old house without so much as turning his head for a peek.

He arrived at Arch's home out of breath, sweat beading up on his forehead. As he pedaled up the drive, Arch pushed the door open and stepped out onto the porch. "Early this morning," he quipped, checking an imaginary watch. "What brings you out so early this morning?"

"Just wanted to get an early start," Joshua panted, waiting for his breath to catch up.

"Well, I'm just ready to fix some hotcakes," Arch said holding the door open. "Want to help or do you need to sit a spell until you catch your breath?"

"No, I mean yes, I mean sure I'd like to help."

They went inside and through to the kitchen. "You know where all the stuff is," Arch said as he cracked eggs into a big crockery bowl. He added buttermilk, flour and the other ingredients, working the batter until he was satisfied. He ladled it onto an iron griddle. "The ancient Greeks were making their version of pancakes called 'tagenites' as early as the 5th century BC," he explained while the cakes began to sizzle. "They were made with wheat flour, olive oil, honey and curdled milk; not much different than what we're eating today wouldn't you say?"

"I think I like pancakes better. How do you know so much stuff?"

"Well, when you have been around as long as I have, you pick up a lot. You been up to anything interesting since you were here last?"

"Nah, just school and stuff."

"Well, I saw a whirligig on the way into town. Strange looking thing though. You must have passed it this morning."

"Oh, yeah, I saw that; but I was going too fast to notice much."

"You know who lives in that house?"

"Na."

"Just wondering. Place looks deserted to me. The pancakes are ready," Arch said, lifting the cakes off the griddle and stacking them high on the platter. "Let's eat 'em while their hot."

After they cleaned up the breakfast dishes, they spent the rest of the morning putting the finishing touches on a large animated whirligig. After lunch, they brought it out from the shop and placed it on a sturdy post. The wind picked up and the whirligig turned to meet the oncoming breeze. As the blades turned, a farmer chopped a log sitting in a cradle. They sat on the porch for a while watching the farmer chop, chop, chop as long as the spring breeze whisked through the yard. Before he left, Joshua helped straighten up the workshop.

On his way home, Joshua had forgotten all about Hobbs until he saw a new whirligig on the post. His eyes anxiously searched for any sign of Hobbs, but to his relief, there was no sign of the man. Two Saturdays passed. Each time Joshua rode home, a new whirligig was perched on Hobbs's fencepost.

He thought about Hobbs and his strange dingy workshop. His conversation with Hobbs twisted in his thoughts. He wondered why couldn't he take a day off like everyone else. Sunday night, Joshua dug through his closet until he found the note. Pulling everything from his back pack, he placed it in the bottom with the cookie crumbs and loose bits of hard candy that had taken up residence through the long school year. Then, he quickly returned the contents, confident the note would be safe from prying eyes.

The note remained in its new hiding place until Tuesday. At lunch, Joshua pulled it from his back pack and carefully examined it. It was perfect in every detail. Hobbs' words pounded in his head. *'Everybody does it. Do they flunk you if you miss a day? They expect you to miss some time. It don't hurt nobody.'* Joshua entered the missing date. At the end of class, he gave the note to Ms. Morgan. That night, Joshua picked at his supper.

"Is something the matter?" his mother inquired.

"Nah, everything's Okay."

"You don't like your supper?"

"Everything's fine, I must've overdone it at lunch."

"I didn't think you were a big fan of school food."

"Sometimes you just want something different, even if it isn't what you really like," Joshua said, stuffing a large forkful of chicken ala king in his mouth. He remained silent for the rest of the meal. Joshua washed up the dishes, then climbed the stairs to his room. He finished his homework and flipped through the cable channels until his mother came to the door.

"Everything alright?" she asked.

"Sure Mom."

"How about a hug before bed?"

"Sure," Joshua said walking over to his mother's outstretched arms. He felt guilty as she pulled him close and kissed his forehead. "G'night Mom."

"G'night dear."

The next morning, Joshua was so anxious, he woke long before his mother. He had stayed in his bed pretending to sleep while she got ready for work. That way, he figured, she could not ask any questions he might have a tough time answering. She was putting on her Super Mart cashier vest, when she called out, "Joshua, time to get up. Gotta go, see you this evening. Your breakfast is in the microwave."

"Okay, Mom."

He waited until he heard the door shut and the car start before getting out of the bed. Soon, he was flying down the road he took every Saturday, the only difference was this day, he was not going to visit Arch.

A new whirligig adorned the fence post at Hobbs's place. Next to it, the scruffy man leaned on the shaky fence. Joshua came to a stop at the driveway. Hobbs pulled a worn pocket watch from his pocket. He flipped open the lid with a touch of his thumb and carefully inspected the timepiece. "Right on time," he sneered, tapping it three times on a bony knuckle. "Didn't bring your toolbox?"

"It would've looked funny if I took it on a school day."

"Smart thinking. You'll get the hang of this yet. Put that behind the house," Hobbs said, pointing to the bike. He walked off. Joshua rolled it over the clumpy, weed choked yard. In comparison to the yard at home, which had already been mowed a couple of times, it looked as if it had not been cut all year. Glancing in the grimy windows as he waded through the growth along the side of the house, he could tell the rooms on this side were still empty. When he reached the shed, he hesitated at the door.

"What's up kid?" Hobbs asked.

"Nothing."

"Then get in here, so's we can talk."

"I just . . ."

"Just what?" barked Hobbs.

"I just thought maybe I should go to school. I'll get a tardy, but at least I won't miss."

"I thought you was smarter than that. What about that note? How ya going to explain that? You made your decision when you handed that note over to your teacher. You can bet she'll ask a lot of questions if you show up now. Questions you can't answer. But, go ahead if you like. You're the one who'll have to answer."

"I guess you're right," Joshua groaned, "It'll just make things worse."

"Listen kid, you gonna mope around all day or are we going to have some fun? I ain't going to wipe your tears all day long. Don't worry, everything will be fine."

After a while, Joshua forgot about the note and skipping school. He and Hobbs spent the day hanging around the shed. They did a little work on some whirligigs, but, for the most part, Joshua listened while Hobbs talked. About noon, Hobbs pulled out his pocket watch. Once again, he tapped it three times on his knuckle, then announced it was time for lunch. Joshua followed him down to the house and through the back door. The hinges called out in pain as Hobbs flung it open. The inside of the house did not look any better than its exterior. The paint was cracked and peeling. In the kitchen, the linoleum was worn through to the subfloor in front of the sink. A refrigerator, covered with greasy fingerprints, hummed in the corner. Paper plates filled a large plastic garbage can next to the door.

Hobbs watched Joshua's reaction. "Sorry kid, maid's year off," he sniggered, rummaging. through the freezer compartment. He tossed a couple of frozen burritos in the microwave. Slamming the door, he pressed the start button, and the unit buzzed to life. Returning to the refrigerator, he pulled out a can of Super Mart NRG Buzz and a beer. He tossed the NRG Buzz to Joshua.

"Here kid, mebbe this will perk you up," he joked. "I bet your mommy won't let you drink this stuff." Joshua nodded in agreement. "Another stupid rule," Hobbs muttered. He pulled the tab on his beer and swilled down a big gulp. The microwave beeped. Popping open the door, he pulled out a burrito and tossed it over to Joshua. "Bon appetite, kid." After they finished eating, Hobbs said, "Just dump your junk in the can on the way out, no muss, no fuss."

The rest of the day, they just sat around. Joshua made a couple of trips to the kitchen for Buzz and beer. Throughout the afternoon, they attacked a stash of munchies which Hobbs had on hand.

It was almost time for Joshua to leave when Hobbs asked, "What's your friend up to these days?"

Joshua, caught off guard, stammered, "Who do you mean?"

"The guy up the road. The whirligig man."

"Oh, you mean Mr. Arch?"

"If that's what he calls himself, yeah."

"Oh, he makes whirligigs like you."

"Really, now."

"Oh yeah, we finished up one last Saturday."

"Well kid, you and I will start one next week."

"Gee, I don't know," Joshua hesitated.

"Oh, let's not go through all that again," said Hobbs. "Tell you what, we'll make a bet. If anyone calls you out on skipping, then I won't ask you again. However, if no one says anything, you come back next week. What d'ya say?"

Joshua thought for a few moments. "OK."

"Thought you might say that," Hobbs sneered, reaching into his pocket. "Here's a note just in case." He held it out for Joshua, who hesitated for a moment then shoved it in his pocket.

Joshua worried all the way home that his mother would find out he had skipped school. Just in case his mother had come home early, he took the long way around so he could come up on his house from the school side. He got off his bike at the bottom of the drive and cautiously walked up to the house. He smiled in relief when he saw their car was not in the drive. Joshua remained on pins and needles for the rest of the night and the next morning. Both passed without incident. His mother acted as if it were any other night. The next morning, Ms. Morgan welcomed him back, telling him he did not have to make up his missed homework assignment.

On his way to see Arch the following Saturday, Joshua was apprehensive over the possibility of another encounter with

Hobbs. It eased when he did not appear. Although Joshua was ashamed that he had skipped school and deceived his mother, he enjoyed the excitement of doing something forbidden. Joshua was finally able to put those thoughts to rest when he saw Arch was waiting for him on the porch. He greeted Joshua with a plate of fritters, doused with powder sugar. They munched on the crunchy treats while Arch enjoyed a coffee and Joshua gulped down fresh squeezed orange juice.

"No history lesson about fritters today?" Joshua asked.

"Sometimes, things taste so good no history lesson is needed."

They finished up the fritters, then headed to the workshop. On the way, Arch asked, "How was school this week?"

"Fine," Joshua said, heart sinking. He did not want to get into a discussion about school.

"Really? I ran into Ms. Morgan at the grocery and she mentioned that you had to miss for some family business." Joshua could feel his cheeks turning red. He looked away in hopes that Arch would not notice. "Nothing serious I hope," added Arch.

"No nothing much, I just sat around all day," Joshua said. In his mind, he tried to convince himself it was not really a lie because that is what he did on Wednesday. He just left out the part about being with Hobbs.

"Well, I'm sure your mother wouldn't take you out of school unless it was important."

"Yeah."

The remainder of the day dragged along for Joshua. He felt bad about his deception, but he was even more afraid of what Arch might think of him if he found out what really happened. He resolved never to skip school again or get tangled up in a knot of lies.

Toward the end of the day, Arch said, "Got a present for you, Joshua." He opened one of the big workshop cabinets and took a bundle of wood from the shelf. "Been collecting this stuff for some time now, and I think it's time to tell you what I have in mind." He placed it on center work table, loosened the knot and let the contents splay out on the table. "I think I've got all the materials and hardware you'd need to make your own whirligig. I want you to have this so you can work on it at home.

"Gee, thanks Mr. Arch. I don't know what to say," Joshua stammered.

"Oh there's one more thing you'll need." Arch said, reaching under the table. "Put this in your tool box. He handed Joshua a push drill. "The bits are stored in the handle. There's one for each size hole you'll need. Now tuck that away in your tool box before you forget and leave it here. I'll tie up all this other stuff good and snug so it won't come apart on your ride home."

They loaded Joshua's bike, double checking the bungee cords to make sure everything was secure. Arch walked with Joshua to the end of the drive. Joshua stopped and stared at the pavement beneath his feet.

"What's up?" Arch asked. "Did we forget something?"

"No," Joshua said softly. "Just wanted to say thanks again." He wanted to tell Arch what had happened on Wednesday, to apologize for his deceit; but fear once again locked his tongue.

"Alright then, see you next Saturday."

As soon as he swung his leg over the seat, Joshua began to dread the ride home. There was no way to avoid passing Hobbs's place. As he approached, his pace slowed to the point he could hardly keep his bike upright. Just as the fence post came into view, he stopped altogether, peering down the deserted road, looking for any sign of Hobbs. Seeing nothing, he got back on his bike and began to pedal frantically in hopes he could blast by before Hobbs appeared. He was flying down the road at top speed, eyes riveted on the fence post when Hobbs stepped out from behind a tree on the opposite side.

"Whoa there, kid," he shouted, holding up his hands. "Where you headed in such a hurry? Ain't got no time for your old friend?"

Joshua came to a skidding stop in the middle of the pavement. He sucked in deep gulps of air as he tried to catch his breath and let his pounding heart slow down. Hobbs placed his boney hands on the handlebars.

"Been up to see the whirligig man?" Hobbs asked, craning his neck to examine the bundle strapped to the bike rack. Stepping around and laying his hand on the bundle he asked, "What we got here?"

"Nothing," stammered Joshua.

"Nothin'? Looks like something to me." Hobbs freed the taut bungee cords that held the bundle. "This bears closer inspection," he hissed, taking it and heading toward his house.

"Hey, give it back," Joshua pleaded.

"Just want to take a look. See what it is. That ain't too much to ask between friends is it?"

"You're not my friend." Joshua snapped. He propped his bike against the fence post and trotted along behind Hobbs. "Now, give it back!"

"All in good time." Hobbs tucked the bundle under his arm, pulling his watch from a tattered pocket. He tapped it three times on his knuckle and opened the face. "All in good time."

When they reached the house, Hobbs sat on the rotting front steps. He tore at the bindings until they lay in shreds at his feet. He dumped the contents out on the ground while Joshua watched in disbelief. Everything Arch had so carefully packed lay scattered on a patch of bare dirt. Hobbs nudged the items around with a scuffed boot. A sneer crawled up one side of his face as he focused in on some wood that had been at the bottom of the pile.

"This should do the trick," he muttered. Reaching down, he picked up the two largest pieces and placed them across his knees. "Been waitin' for this day a long, long time."

"Those are mine," Joshua protested.

"Well of course they are. I propose to change that, however. What'll you take for these?" Hobbs asked.

"Nothing. Mr. Arch gave those to me to build a whirligig."

"That's why I got to have them. Never mind, if it's wood you want, I can provide all you want." He reached over and pried up a section of the front step. Tossing it at Joshua's feet he said, "Here you go."

"I don't want that, I want what Mr. Arch gave me. Besides, why can't you use it?" he said kicking the plank back at Hobbs.

"Cause, I want these, and I aim to have 'em."

"If you don't give 'em back, I'll . . . "

"You'll what?" Hobbs snarled. "Tell your mommy? Tell your precious Whirligig Man? And what'll you tell them? How you lied? How you skipped school? How they can't trust you no more? I bet they'll be real happy to hear all about that. And what will they think of you forging that note and all? If I were you, I'd think twice before I went down that road."

Tears welled up in Joshua's eyes. "Please, I didn't mean to get you in trouble or anything."

"Get me in trouble?" Hobbs laughed. "Trouble's my middle name. You think I give a hoot about what anyone thinks? What're they going to do to me? If I were you, I'd be thinking about what they're going to do to you. Now listen kid, I mean to have this here wood, and that's that. I sure would hate to see you get in a pack of trouble that don't have to happen. Be smart, keep your mouth shut and everything will be just fine."

"What are you going to do with the wood?" asked Joshua.

"Oh, I got plans for it. Been workin' on a special whirligig and this here wood is exactly what I need to finish it up. Ought to be ready next week. Be sure to stop by, and I'll show it to you." He reached in his pocket and drew out a tangled wad of string. Pitching it on the scattered remains of the bundle, he said, "Here you go, use this to tie it back."

He stood up and looked Joshua in the eye. He raised up his hands and snapped a fresh twenty dollar bill between them. The sudden noise startled Joshua.

"Here you go kid," Hobbs cooed, stuffing the bill in Joshua's shirt pocket. "Now we're square. Go buy some comic books or candy bars or something. This ain't no big deal. Keep your mouth shut and no one will be the wiser. Besides, now that I know your price, mebbe we'll do business again sometime." He turned, walked up the steps and disappeared into the dark recesses of the house.

On his way home and throughout the next week, Joshua tried to forget the incident; but, Friday evening arrived without success. He picked at his supper, trying to gather up the courage to tell his mother he had decided to stay home the next day. He wanted to go and spend the day with Arch, but he dreaded the thought of seeing Hobbs.

"I saw Mr. Arch at the Super Mart today," his mother said. "Seemed like he was looking forward to seeing you."

It was then Joshua realized it was just no good. If he told her he was staying home, he would have to make up an excuse, then he would have to tell Arch something and he would never work his way out. "Good," he managed to say.

"Joshua, is something the matter? You've been quiet all week."

"Just been thinking about whirligigs. I haven't figured out what to do yet and Mr. Arch will want to know what I have decided."

"Why don't you make a nice hummingbird?"

"Well, that's an idea; but, I was thinking of something a little more exciting."

"Why don't you ask Mr. Arch for some advice? I'm sure he will help you figure out what to do."

"Yeah, I guess I should do that."

Saturday morning, he set out for Arch's place. As usual for his morning ride, he did not see anything of Hobbs. The day went well enough and to a large extent, Joshua was able to put the thoughts of the past few weeks out of his mind.

At the end of the day, Arch asked, "Have you decided what you are going to do?"

Caught off guard by the question, Joshua asked, "What do you mean?"

"Have you figured out what you are going to make out of the materials I gave you?"

"I don't know yet. Mom said I should ask you. She says I should make a hummingbird."

"Is that what you want?"

"No, not really."

"Well, it's easy enough for me to tell you what to make. However, when you're done, you may find it wasn't really what you wanted. Of course, in the long run, something small like this won't make much difference. But, you'll have more and more decisions to make from here on out."

"You mean about whirligigs?" asked Joshua.

"No, all kinds of things. Some'll be easy, like what to watch on TV. Some'll be hard, like how you'll spend your free time and who you want to hang out with. And some will be darn right tough, like should you stand by while someone gets bullied, or should you cut class. Keep in mind, every decision has a consequence that can turn out good or bad. The trick is to find a way to make the right decision every time. And that's a tall order for anyone. It takes a lot of work; but, it can be done."

"How?" asked Joshua.

"Sometimes," Arch continued, "you'll have to gather a lot of information before you make your decision. Other times, you can tell what to do by the way you feel. Maybe you'll need to talk with someone you trust and who cares about you. Later, as you go through life, you'll know from your experiences what to do. If you think it through, and rely on the right people, you'll make the right decision. But you have to remember, you're always responsible for the decisions you make, so it's always best to make good ones."

"Yeah," said Joshua

"Well, that covers a lot more ground than what whirligig you should make; but, I think it was worth saying. Tell you what, why don't I lend you some of my whirligig books to look through and see if you find something that interests you?"

"Okay," Joshua replied.

Arch opened his large cupboard and retrieved a couple books. "These ought to do," he smiled, handing them to Joshua.

They finish putting the tools away, then swept up the floor. Scooping up the books, Joshua followed Arch back to the house. He placed the books on the bike rack and gently placed his tool box on top. Once they were securely fastened, he said goodbye and started for home. As he approached Hobbs's place, he looked for any sign of the scruffy man. Soon, he was close enough to see the whirligig post and the new contraption which sat upon it. Joshua had intended to pedal as hard as he could along this stretch in an effort to speed by before Hobbs could stop him. Try as he might, his attention was drawn by the whirligig on the post. Joshua felt as if he were trying to pedal through deep, dry sand as he went slower and slower until he was just creeping. He could not take his eyes off of the whirligig. It was a disturbing sight. A gruesome figure towered over a house, arms raised, waiting to smash the structure.

"Waddya think, kid?" Hobbs' harsh voice barked. Startled, Joshua almost fell over, only saving himself by sticking out his leg to steady the bike. Hobbs had appeared out of nowhere, standing right next to him. Joshua's mouth went dry and his heart pounded in his chest. Before he could ride off, Hobbs seized the handlebar. Try as he might, Joshua could not move.

"What's the big hurry? Ain't you interested in my whirligig. Couldn't have made it without you. See that house there," Hobbs rasped, pointing a gnarled finger toward the whirligig. "Made that from the wood you gave me."

"I didn't give you any wood. You stole it from me!" gulped Joshua, finally able to take a breath.

"Ain't stealin' when you pay for it. You decided to keep the money, didn't you? A deal's a deal," Hobbs scoffed. "Take a closer look, kid, mebbe you'll recognize something."

Joshua looked at the whirligig. He examined the menacing figure. Nothing. Then he looked at the building. He leaned closer. In an instant, he recognized it was a replica of Arch's workshop. "How could you?" he screamed reaching out for the whirligig. He wanted to snatch it away.

Hobbs tugged back on the handlebars, pulling Joshua close to his face. "Now, that wouldn't be nice would it, after all the work I put in to it. Couldn't have made it without that nice wood you gave me. Somehow, I don't think your Whirligig Man would appreciate it much though." The leaves in the tree shook as a breeze rushed through. "Storm's a brewin'," he whispered. "Some say, late at night when a gale comes a howlin', whirligigs - they comes to life." The wind gusted, whipping up the road dust. Joshua instinctively shut his eyes and covered his face with his hands to shield it from the stinging grit. After it passed, he opened his eyes to find himself alone on the road. There was no sign of Hobbs or the Whirligig. He remained still for a moment, regaining his composure. Was he dreaming or had this really happened? He searched for any sign of Hobbs or the whirligig. Everything was still. Not wanting to stay any longer under the shadow of Hobbs's place, he left for home.

That evening, Joshua picked at his supper. He did his best to make conversation with his mother, though his thoughts were on the events of the past weeks. He was ashamed he had allowed himself to be duped by Hobbs, that he had let everyone down who mattered to him. He knew eventually the truth would come out. Through the evening, the wind whipped and fat raindrops began to pelt the house. By the time Joshua turned out the light over his bed, rain pelted the roof and thunder rattled the window panes.

He fell into a fretful sleep, a wild dream filling his head. In it, he stood in Mr. Arch's yard. Driving rain stung his face. When the lightning flashed, he could see the workshop. Arch was closing the shutters, his rain slicker flapping in the wind. He closed one set and was moving to another, head bowed against the driving rain. In the dark that followed the lightning flash, a deafening clap of thunder boomed. The lightning flashed again. In its brilliance, Joshua saw the gruesome figure from Hobbs's whirligig towering over the workshop. Huge arms pounded down on the structure, sending shards of wood flying into the air. Under the onslaught, the workshop collapsed on Arch. Through the storm, the gruesome figure continued to pound down on the shattered building.

When Joshua awakened, the storm clouds had cleared and the morning was bright with sunshine. Joshua was unsettled by the lingering images from his dream. He and his mother attended church as usual. After the service concluded, the congregation buzzed with talk about a man who was injured as a result of the storm. Joshua listened for a while before he realized Mr. Arch was the man everyone was talking about. As near as he could tell, he had been taken to the hospital by rescue workers who had found him under the rubble of his destroyed workshop.

On their way home, Joshua and his mother stopped by the hospital to inquire about Arch's status. He had been treated for his injuries and held overnight for observation. Arch was eating some breakfast when they entered his room. His head was wrapped in a thick bandage. Other than that, Josh could not see any other signs of injury.

Arch smiled when he saw them. "Well it's good to see familiar faces," he said softly." For a while, I thought I might spend the rest of eternity underneath my workshop."

"What were you doing out in the storm?" asked Joshua.

"I heard the shutters slamming in the wind and thought I'd close them before they blew away."

"I had an awful dream," said Joshua, "and you were in it. It was just like you said, you were out in the storm closing up the shutters. Then the figure from Hobbs's whirligig started to smash your workshop. You were caught underneath when it fell down."

"An awful dream and as it turns out, an awful experience wasn't it?"

"Mr. Arch, it was all my fault."

"What do you mean?"

I mean I cut school. I went to his house, because he had these whirligigs. He wrote the note for school. But it was me that turned it in. I thought it would be fun to skip school and spend the day hanging around his house. Then when you gave it to me, he said he wanted it to use in his whirligig. I didn't want to give it to him, but I did anyway."

"Gave who what?"

Joshua realized he had finally come to the moment of truth. He could no longer hold his deceit secret in his heart. "The wood that you gave me. The wood to make a whirligig. I let Hobbs take it." Joshua hesitated. "No, I let him have it for twenty dollars."

"Hobbs Hanbi?"

"Yeah, do you know him?"

The smile disappeared from Arch's face. "I've clashed with Hobbs Hanbi for countless years. I know him to be a loathsome serpent, bent on harming all those he encounters. He is consumed with bitterness and hatred. A coward, he tricks the unsuspecting, bending them to his evil purposes. I fear he has done so with you."

Joshua looked away from Arch. "I was worried that you and Mom would find out what I had been doing. I was afraid that you both would be mad at me."

"Joshua, I would not have been mad at you," said Arch, "but, I would have been disappointed that you had lied."

"That would have been worse than you being mad at me," Joshua said, tears welling up in his eyes.

"Joshua, do you remember our discussion about decisions?"

"Yes, but it was too late by then."

"Well, it may have been late for the poor decisions you had already made. However, it's never too late to start making the right decisions, no matter how much it hurts. Now, you're going to have to figure out what you need to do to put things right. I am confident you'll know what to do. Now tell me about this whirligig that Hobbs was intending to build."

"Oh, he built it alright!" Joshua said.

"Okay then, tell me about the whirligig he built."

"Mr. Arch, it was just awful. It had this big ogre-looking thing and when the fan turned, its arms beat down on a little building."

"Describe it."

Joshua hesitated.

"Did it look like my workshop?"

"Yes."

"Was it made out of the wood I gave you?"

"Ye . . .Yes." Joshua stammered.

"So that's how he did it!" exclaimed Arch.

The nurse popped her head in the door and said, "It's time to let Mr. Engel rest. He is a very sick man. You can come back tomorrow and visit some more. I expect he will be here for a long time."

The last thing Arch said before they left was, "Remember what I said Joshua, and you'll know what to do."

It was a quiet ride home. Joshua could see the disappointment in his mother's face. He knew she would talk with him when she was ready. The silence and the look on her face was almost more than he could bear. He wished she would get mad and yell at him so it would all be over. He knew that was not going to happen. Before they reached the turnoff to their street, Joshua summoned up all his courage and said, "Mom, I'm sorry, and I know I don't have the right to ask any favors right now; but, is there any chance we could go to Mr. Arch's house to see what happened?"

"I don't know. You haven't done much lately to warrant a favor."

"Well, it's not really a favor for me. I just want to see if there's anything I can do to help Mr. Arch. I want to see how bad the workshop is. Maybe I can get his tools and stuff cleaned up and put somewhere where they won't be out in the weather. Maybe I can save some of his whirligigs. Maybe that's a way I can start to make up for what I've done."

After a long pause, she said "Well, you're not going to do it in your Sunday clothes. We'll go home first and change."

Joshua was heartbroken when they reached Arch's home and saw the damaged workshop. After his mother parked the car, they walked through the debris until they stood before a gaping hole in the workshop. It looked like a huge fist had torn through the roof and continued right down to the foundation. Despite the damage, Joshua was surprised to find much of the workshop interior unharmed. Only a few whirligigs and Arch's supply of wood scraps were affected.

"I didn't expect this," his mother said. "I don't think there is much we can do."

"But Mom, we can't just leave it like this!"

"I'm sorry, but this is more than we can handle. It's too dangerous and I won't have you end up in the hospital alongside Mr. Engle."

"But Mom," Joshua pleaded.

"No, Joshua. Mr. Engle will just have to let his insurance take care of this. There's nothing we can do. Now let's get back to the car."

"Please, Mom."

"Remember, you are still on thin ice for skipping school, don't push it," she said firmly.

"OK."

On his way back to the car, Joshua spied the anemometer lying on the ground. He picked it up and examined it. The base had been pulled loose from the post. Try as he might, he could not reattach it. "Mom, is it okay if I take this home and see if I can fix it for Mr. Arch?"

"Yes," she said, "Now get in the car."

Joshua had been so upset during the ride to Arch's house, he had forgotten about Hobbs. Now on the way back, he realized that they would have to pass his place. As they neared, Joshua sank lower and lower in his seat. He would have ducked under the dash if he thought he could do it without arousing his mother's curiosity. He cast a furtive glance out the window as they neared Hobbs's driveway. Joshua could see no sign of him. He glanced over at his mother to make sure her eyes were focused ahead and not at the side of the road. When he looked back, Hobbs appeared at the edge of the road. A leering smile cracked across his face. He pointed directly at Joshua, rapping his watch three times on a twisted knuckle. Joshua gasped.

"Did you say something?" his mother asked.

"Didn't you see him?"

"See who, dear?"

Joshua looked back at the spot where Hobbs had appeared. There was no sign of him. "I thought I saw someone by the road: but it must have been a shadow. There's no one there now." They remained silent for the rest of the ride home.

After supper, the silence continued until Joshua and his mother had the long talk he had been dreading. Until then, he had not realized how deeply he had hurt her. If she had simply gotten angry and grounded him for a week or two, he could have handled it. The sadness in her voice crushed him. All this was amplified by the fact his father, before he left on his tour of duty, had asked Joshua to take care of his mother. Now, he felt he had betrayed his father too. After the talk, he went up to his room, buried his face in his pillow and cried.

Another long talk waited the next day, this time with Ms. Morgan. She, like his mother and Arch, expressed disappointment in what he had done. She also sentenced him to serve some detention as well as lose credit for skipping.

A few days passed before Joshua's thoughts turned to the anemometer he had rescued from Arch's yard. He went outside and picked it up from the table on the porch where he had laid it the day he and his mother had helped with the clean-up at Arch's workshop. Plunking down in the old wicker rocker, he examined it again, holding it up so the breeze could catch the brass cups. They began to spin around. He looked at the base. The flat, bronze mounting plate was warped. Joshua reckoned it could be easily flattened by standing it on the concrete step and tapping it with his hammer. Then, all that would be needed were four sturdy screws to replace those that had been lost.

His thoughts turned to his conversation with Arch in the hospital. He wondered why Arch had been so interested in Hobbs's whirligig? It was as if Arch had known what the little building looked like, that it had been made from wood from his workshop. He also wondered what. Arch meant when he said 'So that's how he did it!'?

Thoughts whirled in his head. He remembered what Hobbs had said. 'Some say, late at night when a gale comes a howlin', whirligigs - they comes to life.' Just then, a whirlwind swept through the yard, momentarily picking up leaves and dust before it dissipated. Joshua bolted up from the chair and dashed into the house. He raced up the stairs to his bedroom and flung open the closet door. Pulling his desk chair inside, he stood on the seat, reaching to the back corner of the shelf. He retrieved a small cardboard box, tore off the lid and snatched up the twenty dollar bill Hobbs had given him. He had a plan for his whirligig.

By Friday evening, Joshua had finished his whirligig. He suspended it from the arms of the repaired anemometer he had placed on a fence post in the back yard.

"Mom, come see it," he called out.

She stepped out from the kitchen. "What is it?" she asked looking at the lumpy grey papier-mâché funnel. "Looks like a beehive you'd find hanging from a tree limb."

"Not quite, Mom; but, that might do." Joshua gave it a spin. "Now?"

"A cocoon?"

"No, again."

"Well, are you going to tell me?"

"I think it's more fun to let you guess. Wait until it gets going and maybe you can figure it out." The air remained still and the grey lump sat motionless.

"They're forecasting a storm tonight, you better not leave that out." she warned.

"That's just what I'm hoping for."

"Suit yourself, but don't come crying to me if it's all torn up in the morning."

"I won't," Joshua said confidently.

"Come in for supper," she said walking back into the house.

Joshua followed. He set out the plates and silverware while she filled bowls and platters with food. They went through the usual routine until it was time for Joshua to go up to his room. He plopped down on his bed wondering what would become of his whirligig that night.

He fell asleep as the wind picked up, its rushing sound filling his head. Joshua dreamed he stood in the entrance of Hobbs's driveway. The wind whipped through the trees. They creaked and groaned as an invisible hand of air pushed them to the breaking point. Lightning split the sky. In its brilliant flash, he could see Hobbs standing on the porch of his house. It shook violently in the gusting wind. A scowl crawled across his face. Darkness followed, accompanied by the angry growl of thunder. The roar continued like the sound of an oncoming freight train bearing down at full throttle. Lightning flared across the sky again. In its radiance, Joshua saw a churning grey funnel engulf the house and Hobbs. The deafening sound of splitting wood combined with the Hobbs's gruesome howl continued until the next blaze of lightning revealed an empty field.

Just before dawn, the wind calmed and quiet settled over Joshua's dreams. The image of the Hobbs being sucked up into the black sky remained in his mind. After breakfast, he went outside. To his dismay, the anemometer was gone. He couldn't believe it had been completely carried off by the wind. He frantically searched for any sign of it. His mother came out to help.

"I warned you this might happen," she said in a soothing voice, "though I didn't think the whole thing would end up missing." She put a comforting arm around his shoulder. "Listen, I've got some news for you. Mr. Engle just called. He's been released from the hospital. He asked if you could come over to his place. I told him you were grounded." She shot Joshua a stern look waiting to see if he had any reaction. "He said he really needed to talk with you." Joshua looked back to see if there was any hope of seeing Arch. "I told him you could, provided you went there and back and no place else. Agreed?"

"You bet!"

"He said not to pack your bike because he'll pick you up in a few minutes. What will you tell Mr. Engle about his anvil monitor?"

"Anemometer, Mom, and I will tell him the truth. I've learned my lesson."

As happens most often after storms at night, the morning was bright and sunny. Joshua sat on the porch until Arch pulled up the drive. He was glad Arch was out of the hospital, and hoped he would feel good enough to start repairing the workshop. Joshua put his toolbox in the bed of the truck and climbed in the passenger side. He enjoyed the ride, asking all about the hospital.

"I thought the nurse said you would be in the hospital a long time," Josh said.

"So she did and so I thought. Guess you could say I had a miraculous recovery."

For the rest of the trip, Arch answered all Joshua's questions about hospital food and how many shots he got and whether they hurt or not. He was just about to explain about the anemometer when they stopped in front of Arch's home. Joshua realized he had not even noticed when they passed by Hobbs's place. Flashes of his dream popped into his head. He wondered how Hobbs had fared during the storm.

Grabbing his toolbox, Joshua followed Arch through the yard to the workshop. To his amazement, there was no sign of the damage that took place just a week earlier. He ran ahead and swept his hand over the wall where the gaping hole had been.

"Unbelievable!" he cried.

"Yes, it is quite remarkable. Just like it never happened. Another miraculous recovery I would say."

"When'd it get fixed? The last time I saw it, it was in pretty bad shape."

"Early this morning. Let's go inside and inventory everything and see if it is all there." They went inside and spent the rest of the morning checking every tool and whirligig.

"I could swear this one was all torn up," Joshua declared, holding up a whirligig with a man in a row boat. "And that one too," he said, pointing to a swan. "Looks like they are all here. I don't understand."

"Maybe everything made a miraculous recovery. What's important is that they are all here now. How about some lunch and then I'll need to get you back home," Arch said heading out the door. Joshua followed.

They had gone just about half way when Joshua called out, "Wait, I just remembered, I have to tell you about the anemometer!"

"What about it?" Arch asked, stepping to one side so Joshua could see it spinning around atop its ornate mast. "Looks fine to me."

Joshua's jaw dropped as he watched the brass cups twirling round and round. "But, I . . . I . . ."

"Yes, I know," Arch said. "You borrowed it and now it's back. Thank you for straightening the mounting plate. Come on, I'm hungry for something that's not hospital food." Joshua didn't say a word while Arch fixed lunch. Finally after the dishes had been cleaned and they sat on the porch, Joshua spoke of his experiences with Hobbs. He also explained about the whirligig he made.

"So you made a papier-mâché tornado. Ingenious!" Arch chuckled. "And what became of the twenty dollar bill?"

"I mixed it in with the newspaper when I made the papier-mâché. I figured out why Hobbs wanted the wood from your workshop so badly. His whirligig wouldn't work unless it had something of yours. So I figured I would return the favor with the twenty he gave me."

"Did it work?"

"I don't know, we went by so fast this morning, I forgot to look."

"Well, it's time to be heading back anyway, let's stop on the way."

The ride to Hobbs's lasted far too long to suit Joshua. He strained to see as far down the road as he could, willing Arch's truck to go faster. Finally, they arrived. Arch pulled the truck into the drive and stopped. Joshua hopped out of the truck and ran through the weed choked yard to the rotting steps of the house. The roof was caved in allowing the sunlight to shine down on the rotting innards of the crumbling house. Joshua ran around back. There, he found a tumble of planks where Hobbs's shed had been. The back wall of the house was caved in, exposing the kitchen area. The plaster on the walls had disintegrated leaving sun bleached slats clinging to warped studs. Large holes gaped in the floor.

Arch joined him. "I don't think anyone is here," he said.

"I don't understand."

"Understand what?" Arch asked.

"This doesn't look like a tornado hit it. It looks like it's been abandoned for years. It didn't look like this a week ago, but this is where he was," Joshua protested. "I know he was."

"I'm sure he was. You've got to remember, though, with a creature like Hobbs, things aren't always what they seem. You see, Hobbs thrives on lies and trickery. When that doesn't work anymore, he packs up and goes. I'm sure he's long gone from here by now."

"Will he come back?"

"No, Once he's been defeated, he won't come back. He'll go somewhere else looking for mischief. Come on, let's go before your mother gets worried. She's got something important to tell you."

"What's that?"

"Well it wouldn't be right for me to spoil her surprise. But, there is something I need to tell you while we ride." They walked back to the truck and were soon on their way. They sat in silence for a while before Arch finally spoke up. "Joshua, the time has come for me to move along."

"What do you mean?"

"I mean it is time for me to leave this place. I've done what I was sent here to do. Hobbs is bound to set up shop somewhere else and it's up to me to find out where and stop him. It's not going to be easy for me to leave, because I have grown attached to you and your mother and all the other good folks I have met while I've been here. "

Joshua sat in stunned silence. Tears welled up in his eyes. He tried to hold them back, but they poured out and ran down his cheeks. He angrily wiped them away with the sleeve of his shirt.

"But you can't."

"I must."

"I don't want you to go." Joshua pleaded.

"Joshua, you will have to trust me on this. Things will work out." Arch said reaching over and touching his shoulder. Immediately, a sense of calm settled over Joshua.

"If you say so, but, I'm having a hard time believing it right now."

"You will soon."

They pulled up the driveway. Joshua's mother, who had been looking out the window, rushed from the kitchen and down the steps to meet the truck. Joshua opened the door and stepped into the open arms of his mother. She hugged him tightly as tears rolled down her face.

"Mom?"

"Oh Joshie, I just got the very best news ever."

"What's that, Mom?"

"Joshie, they found your father. He's coming home. He's coming home." She hugged him so tight he thought she would squeeze the breath right out of his lungs. The tears of disappointment he had been holding back now became tears of joy and he let them stream out and roll down his cheeks. He looked around to share the good news with Arch only to find the driveway was empty.

PRYDWEN FAR

Arthur sat back in the recliner, staring into the blackness that filled his field of vision. It was a perfect blackness. Like the blackness he remembered as a boy on a school field trip to the Lewis & Clark Caverns. Deep inside, the guide turned off the lights leaving them in total darkness – pitch darkness. The black was absolute, impenetrable.

Tris had not moved since Arthur had floated him up from the stasis hold. *Was he somehow affected? Will he ever wake up? Maybe the real question is: am I awake or just dreaming all this?*

He engaged his console button activating the convex semicircle of cushioned recliners. They began to rotate inside the perimeter of the observation pod. As they did, the Universe, at least what he guessed was the Universe, slid into sight. The recliners floated so gently over a maglev track, he could easily imagine that everything outside was rotating around him. When he stopped half way around, the splendor of the Universe spread out before him. A never-ending wall of onyx, encrusted with a myriad of stars and galaxies.

It reminded Arthur of summer nights, back in Montana, during a new moon. He and his brother, Wayne, would climb Painted Rocks in the West Fork Valley of the Bitterroot Mountains. The two would lie on their backs, watching the Milky Way glide across the sky. They talked of baseball, girls and life. Only this was not Painted Rocks and there was no Milky Way rising up from the horizon. Arthur knew Wayne was somewhere out there, near one of those specks of light. *But which one?*

When he had first come up to the observation pod, the panorama seemed evenly split between blackness and Universe.

He had been rotating the chairs between the two, trying to make sense of what he was seeing. He wished Tris would wake. *Could he explain what was going on?*

Tris began to rouse from his stasis syncope. Opening his eyes, he saw the Universe spread out before him. He gasped, "What the hell?"

"Easy Tris," said Arthur, "you're in the observation pod."

"Why?"

"Apparently, there's been some malfunction. Emergency protocol must have been triggered, and I, as expedition leader, was brought out of stasis first to make an assessment."

"Well, what did you find?'

"There aren't enough diagnostics on line to indicate anything definitive. I don't think we have a hull breach as we obviously still have breathable atmosphere. I can't tell if the gravity inverters are functioning. It's possible the Prydwen is running on battery reserve."

Tris leaned forward and turned his head in the direction of Arthur's voice, in an attempt to see his face in the starlight. "Well if all that is true, what the hell did you bring me up here for? Why aren't we trying to find out what's happened? Seems to me that would be a better plan than taking a break in the observation room."

"Since the diagnostics are out, I thought perhaps I could see if there was any visible damage to the gravity inverters from up here." He nudged the console button, tilting the observation pod down until a 500 foot long boom, stretching out toward the stars, came into view. It enclosed 20 gimbals, each containing one ten-sided gravity inverter. Even at 20 feet in diameter, they were barely discernable in the dim starlight.

Tris squinted, hoping to improve the visibility. "I guess they look alright. Can't see any obvious damage. They all seem aligned for maximum hyperlight velocity. What about the rest?" Arthur initiated rotation. The boom, followed by the Universe, slid out of their field of vision. Tris watched in silence as it was replaced by blackness. "I don't understand. What's happened?"

"Your guess is as good as mine," said Arthur, "but, I believe it can be only one of two situations."

"Go on!"

"Something happened that kept us from stopping at our intended destination. That much is clear. It's possible we just kept going. Travelling ahead until we reached the edge of the Universe."

"I'm not buying it," said Tris. "The farthest galaxy we know of is trillions of astronomical units from earth. That's over a billion light years. You want me to believe something happened and we just kept going – blissfully sleeping in stasis - until we ended up at the edge of the Universe? Even at hyperlight speeds, that would take an awfully long time."

"Maybe not. Theoretically, there is no top end to the amount of dark gravity the inverters can generate. If that is true, then there is no limit when travelling in hyperlight. The Prydwen's speed could have increased until movement between points, no matter how far apart, was virtually instantaneous. A malfunction could have kicked them into maximum drive."

"And so, what then? We reached the edge of the Universe and we just stopped?"

"I'm not sure we have stopped."

"What do you mean?"

"Before I get into that, if I have judged correctly and rotated us 180 degrees, the other half of the boom should be straight ahead. Take a close look and tell me if you see anything."

Tris searched the blackness. His eyes picked up the faintest hint of starlight that was now behind them, reflecting off the boom. "Yes, I see."

"When I first came up here, that reflection was much stronger. That can mean only one thing. We are moving away from the source of light."

"Away from the Universe?"

"Yes."

"Arthur, presuming the gravity inverters are still functional, can't we put them in reverse and go back?"

"Ay, there's the rub. The inverters rely on gravity, the stuff of all things in the Universe, from atoms to galaxies and even light itself. It may well be the most plentiful thing within the Universe. In this other place, I fear a dearth of it. As the Prydwen moves beyond the Universe and away from gravity, the less fuel there is for the inverters. They may have already sputtered out and our momentum keeps us ever moving away. That is, if any of the laws of physics as we understand them, apply here."

"This is starting to scare the hell out of me."

"Can't say I'm all that comfortable with the concept myself."

"Well, we have to try something!" cried Tris.

"What do you suggest? Do you have a bag of Pixie Dust handy? Perhaps we could sprinkle it about and fly home."

"This is no time for jokes."

"You're right, I apologize," said Arthur. He tilted the observation pod up while he rotated it to face the Universe. It now had a defined shape. The bright crystal points of light suspended in black they had seen just moments before were now glowing fuzzy spots suspended in a pale milky blob, corralled by encroaching blackness.

"How far do you have to travel for the Universe to look so small?" asked Tris.

"I couldn't begin to guess," Arthur said, tilting the observation pod down. The tip of the inverter encroached the bottom of the ball of light as a tiny black smudge. "Soon, the Universe will be too small for us to see anything of the boom. If it is there at all."

"What do you mean?"

"I said there were two situations which could explain what is happening. You have heard the first. Before I share the second, I'd like to know if you have formed any hypothesis."

Tris hesitated. "I can't think of anything. All this is making my head smoke. Go on."

"It is evident under the circumstances of my first scenario, there is little we can do regarding our situation. I know that's not what you want to hear. If that indeed is our plight, we will just have to ride it out until we eventually die in the blackness of this other place."

"Is that the good news or the bad news?"

"Let me tell you the other possible explanation and then you can decide."

"Am I going to like this any better?"

"Probably not."

"Shoot."

"I think it's possible the boom may not be there, nor the Universe," Arthur said, pointing toward the blob of light, "because nothing may be there – nothing may be here. Maybe we're not here. What if something horribly wrong took place and we died and this is just the residual of our conscious energy fading away?"

"That's it, we blew up or something and we just fade away. What about God? I thought there would be Heaven or Hell or something more than this when the time came."

"That may still await us. Perhaps we are just in some transition. Either way, it seems we'll just have to ride it out to its conclusion." Arthur peered at the shrinking blob of light. "Tris, I can't remember what the night sky at home looked like. Or the mountains, or my brother's face for that matter."

Tris tried to recall familiar images. Nothing. "Me either. Does this mean our memories of the Universe are fading away as the residual of our conscious energy fades away?"

"Maybe. Or perhaps the memories of us are fading away from the Universe."

NATURAL CAUSES[4]

"Come in Ludlow," Okoro said, eyeing his novice field operative. *So pale, must come from an isolated area. Perhaps even a separatist pure gene enclave.* "Your incident report?" he asked, not needing to pose a direct question.

"Yes sir," Ludlow responded. He walked forward and stood before the sprawling desk of the Wooton Outlands Exploration Chief of Security. He made sure to maintain eye contact with the imposing man, who remained seated. "E-riginal uploaded to your personal eyes-only system, and here are my portmedia E-logs as specified by protocol." He held out his hand, offering Okoro a digichrys.

Okoro studied the young field operative, looking for the smallest minim of body language, any fleeting micro-twitches of facial muscles, hoping to discern any subconscious signal of emotional anxiety or distress. *What are you thinking after your first assignment?* He paused before taking the digichrys from Ludlow's outstretched hand. *Hand steady, no tells there.* "And Tpecka?"

"With the med-techs."

"Preliminary findings?" Okoro continued without pausing.

"None as of yet," Ludlow replied.

"And the resource station?"

"Swept and secured. The replacement op arrived just as I was finishing."

"Tpecka's personal effects?"

---

[4] "Natural Causes" appeared on line in *Chronoscope Magazine*, 12/29/2016.

"Retrieved. Not much really, uniforms, sundries and the like. A fairly Spartan existence as near as I could tell. Not much of a life out there, at least not for Tpecka."

Okoro perceived a slight dilation in Ludlow's pupils. "First time out?"

"Yes sir."

"Indeed, not much of a life out there." Okoro paused, eyes locked on the young man, providing an opportunity for him to speak. *Finally, the shoulders slump.*

"Sir," Ludlow began hesitantly, "there weren't any photographs or personal transmissions in the system. It just seems that Tpecka would have had something of family or friends about. After all, minimum on site assignments are two years. That's an awful long time to be alone on some desolate planet."

Okoro motioned to a single chair at the corner of the desk. "Sit down."

Ludlow sensed it was not an offer, but still hesitated, not wanting to appear presumptuous. However, his legs, now feeling the weight of the retrieval mission settling in, convinced him to take a seat.

"Station Log?" Okoro continued once Ludlow was settled.

"All seems in order, sir."

"Personal log?"

"One digichrys found. It's with Tpecka's personal effects."

"And the contents?"

"Downloaded to a secure personal and confidential server. Diagnostic comparison to station log and data run."

"Results?"

"There were anomalies from almost the beginning, but in the absence of a diagnostic comparison of all data, too insignificant to raise any flags. In hindsight analysis, there appears to be a steady increase in both frequency and magnitude.

As we approach the incident, they become recognizably dramatic." Ludlow paused, hoping Okoro would provide a prompt. The Chief Security Officer obliged by waving a hand over the desk top. Ludlow continued, "Cyrrhestes 4 incident anomaly analysis." The images of tropical fish swimming on the wall were replaced by a list of dates and identification numbers. Ludlow fished his handheld from the utility pocket of his jumpsuit and tapped a few times on the screen. "I have examined the anomalies identified by diagnostics and suggest we concentrate on the last few days before the incident, that is, of course, unless you want to examine all of them."

"Proceed."

"The first one I have selected occurred ten days before Tpecka's last transmission." Ludlow tapped the handheld and the wall screen displayed the voice log transcript. "Seems normal enough," he continued. "Tpecka reports that the station temperature is above normal despite the fact the thermostat shows normal." He tapped the handheld again. More data appeared on the wall. "Station data records indicate that the ambient temperature is at the specified setting. Outside temperature recorded was also within normal range. By itself, this could be explained by any number of factors, none of which would be much cause for concern."

"Personal log?"

Ludlow brought up the transcript.

"Voice recording." Okoro could see Ludlow's neck muscles tighten even before he turned. *You weren't expecting that, were you.*

One look at Okoro's steady gaze told Ludlow the request was no mistake. He quickly swiped over to the voice recording screen and brought up the recording. It started with the computer generated universal date/time stamp followed by the voice of Iskra Tpecka.

> **'Open personal and confidential log. It seems so hot in the station. The thermostat says the temperature is 21°, but it feels warmer. Completed all my tasks for this duty period but there is still some time before the shutters close. Perhaps there will be some relief from this heat once the light is shut out. Until then, there is little to do but listen to the wind and look at the dunes. They remind me of White Sands. I hope I can sleep in this heat. Close log.'**

Okoro held up a hand, signaling Ludlow to pause. *The timbre in the voice. Definitely a fair amount of distress.* "Did you hear that?"

"What sir? Was there something in particular?"

"Learn to listen not only to the words but to the special character, the distinguishing quality of the voice. In that, you will find revealed the person. There was more on Tpecka's mind than the temperature."

Ludlow struggled to formulate what would pass for an intelligent response. "I see how that would prove useful in my duties, sir."

"In everything."

"Yes sir, shall I continue?"

Okoro nodded.

Ludlow began, wondering what Okoro was reading in his voice. "Station metrics from this date show all systems functioning within normal parameters. According to the readouts, the temperature recorded inside was a constant 21°. No interruptions in power, no external solar disturbances. It's much the same for the next few days. Normal station metrics but P&C

logs full of complaints about the heat. " Ludlow queued the next recording. "This one is five days from the log we just heard:

'Open personal and confidential log. There is no relief from the heat. Has to be a malfunction somewhere in the system. The thermostat says its 21° but it must be at least 30°. Readouts must be off too. Put in a request to Control for assistance. Haven't been able to sleep much in all this heat. In the desert, it cools off at night, but there's no night here, just the glare of Cyrrhestes. Close log.'

"Records show that Tpecka did send a request for assistance. Control ran remote diagnostics and determined that all station systems were functioning within normal parameters which agreed with station metrics. Since the distance between Cyrrhestes 4 and Control is 12 Astronomical Units, the response arrived after the incident occurred.

"This next log is from a day later:

'Open personal and confidential log. Control hasn't responded to my requests. The heat is almost unbearable. I can't eat, can't sleep. Today I tried a manual override on the air conditioning system. Turned the temperature as low as the settings would allow. Nothing. I feel trapped in here. Close log.'

"Records confirm a manual override of the station's HVAC to the lowest setting was initiated on this date. Subsequently, the temperature inside dropped to 15°." Ludlow turned to look at Okoro.

Okoro studied Ludlow's face. *So you have a question not quite on topic.* "Is there something else?".

"What qualifications did Tpecka have for this job?"

"A fair question." Okoro passed a hand over the desk top and said, "Tpecka." Immediately, a dossier flashed on the wall screen. Okoro summarized the contents for Ludlow. "Orphaned in the Fyro Macedonia uprising, she ended up in a Mediterranean Federation Displaced Persons Camp. There, evaluations revealed her IQ to be in the top 100th percentile. She was bid out to Catholic Charities. At age 16, she received a scholarship to Katholieke Universiteit Leuven. Followed that with a PhD in physics and astronomy from ETH Zurich. At age 21, became the youngest appointee to the Federation Space Exploration Academy at White Sands. Bright future, wouldn't you say?"

"No disrespect to the company sir, but someone with a resume like that doesn't end up in a dead end job on Cyrrhestes 4. . ." Ludlow countered.

"Indeed. Do you have more for me?" Okoro asked, diverting the line of discussion.

"This short log was recorded just 3 days before the incident:

'Open personal and confidential log. No relief from the heat. Went outside to check the mechanicals. Even the damn envirosuit is busted. Roasted in it. I'm too exhausted to continue. Close log.'

"Station data shows the envirosuit was activated. I found it on the floor. In addition, the data confirms the station hatch as well as the outside mechanical room hatch were actuated. Metrics indicate the suit was fully functional within normal parameters. Onsight tests confirm this. I inspected the mechanicals and found everything in good order and functioning properly." Ludlow paused. "It gets even stranger. This is the log from the following day:

'Open personal and confidential log. Disabled the shutters. Can't stand to look outside. Too much like White Sands; just endless, empty dunes. Close log.'

"Sir, the shutters were disabled, but in the open position. Every one, in every room. Servos disconnected. It's clear Tpecka had some serious problems. Don't they screen candidates for this job?" Ludlow looked Okoro straight in the eyes. *Did I see a small twitch?*

Okoro drew in a measured breath. "Wooton is not without its methodology to select candidates for resident operators. It should come as no surprise that individuals with minimal or no family associations are preferred for assignments of this nature. Couple that with an education like Tpecka's and it's easy to see how a junior grade HR recruiter would be disposed to consider her an outstanding candidate.

"There is more to her story that won't be found in Tpecka's general personnel file. While you were onsite, I did some digging. Seems that in the midst of all her Academy studies, she managed to acquire a fiancé. While not prohibited by the Academy, such attachments were highly scrutinized. Just before graduation, Tpecka treated her sweetheart to a night out at a Greek ouzerie to celebrate his birthday. They were on their way home when she lost control of the car. She was thrown free, but he was trapped in the burning wreckage. He lingered a month in the burn ward before he died. Blood alcohol tests revealed she was just under the legal limit, but she was dismissed from the Academy anyway. Washed out, she bounced around from position to position on the periphery of the space industry, never able to latch on to anything long term. Some years later she checked herself into rehab citing mental exhaustion. Seems she blamed herself for her fiancé's death. A couple of years later, she came out with a clean bill of health. As for official records, The Academy, preferring to avoid controversy, simply noted Tpecka was found not to be suited for duty. As for her rehab, antiquated HIPPA regulations blocked access to her medical files. But as you will find, there's nothing sacred that a little cash and coercion can't fix. Anyway, the rest you know."

Ludlow slumped in his chair. He tapped his handheld. "That may well explain her last log entry:

'Open personal and confidential log. Today is Rick's birthday. I fixed him a cake and even put candles on it, but they melted. I think I'll take a nap before I join him. Close log.'

"Data confirms the station hatch was engaged just after this entry. The sensors lost vitals after that, prompting the need for an onsite investigation. I arrived a month later. When I approached the hatch, the outer door was open. Fortunately, the inner door was closed. I searched the station thoroughly, but didn't find Tpecka. I took my search outside where I found her lying in the snow around the side of the building. She didn't have a stitch of clothing on, not even boots. Frozen stiff as you would expect. Temperature outside that day was minus 100°. Even at that temperature, I guess it took awhile for her to freeze. It looked like she had just curled up for a nap. Anyway, I placed her in a body bag. I secured the station and a week later handed the keys over to the replacement op and returned. It's all in my report.

"As for the body, I made sure it stayed frozen at minus 100° until I turned her over to the med-techs." Ludlow's headset pinged. "Excuse me sir, I asked the med-techs to call me with the findings as soon as they completed their examination."

Okoro nodded.

Ludlow tapped the module. A thin mic glided out from the unit, stopping just at the corner of his mouth. "Go ahead." He listened intently, then asked, "Are you sure? No way!" He waited for a response. "You have verified all the information and you have no doubts. . . You really want me to tell him that? . . . Alright, I'll tell him." He tapped the module again and the mic receded. "Sir, the med-techs have completed the autopsy." He hesitated, searching for the right words.

"Go on," Okoro said impatiently.

"I don't know how to put this sir, it goes against all reason."

"What are you talking about?"

"The results –"

"Yes, go on!"

"I know this is going to sound ridiculous. I feel foolish even repeating what the med-techs have told me."

"Get to the point, Ludlow. I want to wrap this up."

"As you wish. I know this is going to sound crazy, but the med-techs say their examination reveals Tpecka's internal organs suffered extensive damage consistent with heat stroke. Like she had roasted to death from the inside. They're waiting to hear from you before they enter the cause of death." *Is that a bead of sweat on your temple?*

Okoro folded his hands together, taking in a measured breath. For some time, he leaned back in his chair, staring at the ceiling. Finally, he said, "Ludlow, like all institutions, Wooton Outlands Exploration prefers tidy explanations that do not raise eyebrows or beg further investigation. Best tell the techs to adjust the record to show Tpecka died of Natural Causes."

A NEW LEAF[5]

Stan was pouring a fresh cup of coffee in the breakroom when his mobile rang. He dug the phone out of his pocket and checked the screen. *Leif. First thing Monday morning. What now?*

Stan touched the screen. "What do you want?"

"I need you to come get me."

"What's going on? You still sobering up?" *Ten minutes until start time. The sonofabitch. Always cutting it too close for comfort.*

"I'm here at Hava Java. I was grabbing a latté and my car died."

"Why don't you walk? It's not that far."

"Can't risk it. You know what'll happen if I miss any more work. Morton will be on my butt like honey on a biscuit."

"Yeah, I expect the old man would stretch your hide on a rack if you were late again." Stan did a quick mental calculation. "Okay, I should have time. Let me get my keys and I'll come get you. Be out front. I don't want to have to go looking for you."

"I'll owe you for this." The call disconnected.

Stan left the break room and headed for the cubical pen down the hall. As he navigated through the stalls, he noticed someone in Leif's.. To his utter surprise, his friend was there as big as life, taking a sip from a large, steaming Hava Java cup. *Another one of his stupid pranks! Should'a known better.* He stopped when he reached the cubical.

"Busted! You almost had me this time."

Leif smiled. "Good morning, Stan. How are you?"

"Oh, you're cool, buster. Acting like nothing happened."

---

[5] "A New Leaf" was accepted for publication by *Storyteller*, 9/2017

"Sorry Stan, hold that thought. I need to put the finishing touches on the Boursaw report before I send it to Mr. Morton." He returned to his typing. Stan snuck a peek at his monitor in hopes of seeing what porn site Leif was on. To his surprise, there were no naked women on the screen nor even a game of War Babies. He was actually sending an email to Morton. Leif clicked on the send button. "There. Now, what was it you were saying?"

"I thought you said that wasn't due till tomorrow."

"Yes."

"It's not like you to get anything done on time, much less early."

"No time like the present. Is there something you wanted? If it's not urgent, how about we talk at break? I want to get a leg up on the financials."

Stan shook his head. *That son-of-a-gun is up to something. Best leave it alone and not play into his hands.*

"No, it's not important. Catch you later." He left Leif busily typing. Whatever he was up to, it didn't seem to follow Leif's typical bonehead approach, which not only extended to his sophomoric pranks, but to life in general. Stan settled in at his desk and turned on his computer. A few minutes later, his cell phone rang.

Now what? He checked the display. It was Leif.

"What?"

"Where the hell are you? I thought you were coming to get me," Leif complained.

"I thought you were too busy working on financials."

"How can I work on the financials when I'm here waiting on you?"

"Give it a rest, Leif." Stan disconnected. Leif could be exhausting. Often times, Stan thought he was just a big kid running around in a thirty-five-year-old man's body.

About forty-five minutes later, Stan was startled to hear Leif's panting voice in his left ear. "Fine friend you are, butt wad. I ask one little favor from you to save my bacon and you hang up on me. Do you realize I had to hoof it all the way up here from Hava Java? If I get fired, it's your fault."

Stan turned in his chair to see a disheveled Leif glaring at him. Perspiration beaded up on his forehead. "No, if you get fired it's your fault. But you're not getting fired this morning: that is, not unless you have done something stupid in the last few minutes. Give it up, Leif. Your trick didn't work, and no amount of play acting will change that. I found you out, so just get over it. Now, if you don't mind, I've got my own work to finish. By the way, nice effect with the fake perspiration on the forehead."

"What the hell do you mean, 'found me out'?"

"To start with, just after your first call, I found you sitting at your desk. Early for a change, I might add. We actually had a normal conversation. Next, it doesn't take forty-five minutes to walk up here from Hava Java." Stan folded his arms and stared at Leif.

"First of all, I had to finish my coffee before I started. Couldn't risk spilling it. Second of all, I couldn't have been at my desk, because I've been walking up here since you blew me off. That's why it took forty-five minutes." Leif glared at Stan.

"I can prove you were here."

"I dare you!"

"If I do, will you promise to shut up for the rest of the day?" Stan was ready to set the hook.

"Yeah."

"And promise no more stupid pranks -- ever?" Stan knew it would never happen.

"Okay, but if you can't, you'll finish the Boursaw proposal for Morton that's due tomorrow. Agreed?"

Stan smiled. *Got you now, dumbass.* "Agreed. Come on." He made a beeline to Leif's cubicle. "Have you been to your computer yet?" Stan asked, as they reached Leif's cubical.

"No."

"Well, how do you explain that?" Stan pointed to the monitor. It was open to Leif's work dashboard.

"Somebody must have turned it on."

"Who knows your password other than you?"

Leif stared at the monitor. "Dunno."

"Nobody, that's who. Now, check your sent email."

Leif sat down. He clicked on the email icon and opened the sent folder. The display listed five emails sent within the last forty-five minutes, including one with an attachment to Morton. Taking a deep breath, he sat back in his chair, covering his eyes with his hands. "It can't be. Someone must have hacked into my computer."

"Yeah, a hacker busted into your computer and got all your work caught up for you."

"It does sound crazy."

"Yes it does. I'll give you credit for trying, but a bet's a bet. Don't push your luck. I'm a little miffed that you've made me waste a pretty good chunk of my morning screwing with your nonsense. I need to get back to my work. And no more pranks. Okay?"

"Okay," said Leif sheepishly.

* * *

Two weeks had passed when Stan stopped by Leif's cubicle. "What's up? You've been mighty quiet the past couple of weeks. You still pissed about the Hava Java thing?" Stan saw the beard stubble and bloodshot eyes. Leif's shirt looked like it had just been retrieved from the laundry basket – before it had been washed.

"No." Leif scowled. "Why should I be upset my best friend blew me off and left me stranded at the coffee shop?" He paused. "Are you still pissed?"

"Ancient history." Stan spied Mr. Morton making a beeline for Leif's cubicle. *This can't be good.* He looked for a way to exit gracefully, but Morton had him blocked.

"Lee, my boy," Morton said, peering over the top of Leif's cubicle. "Just wanted to have a short chat about the Boursaw proposal."

"That's Leif, Mr. Morton."

"That was some good work you did, not like your usual offerings," Morton continued. "We got the contract."

"You'll never know how much I put into that proposal, Mr. Morton."

"Well, I hope this signals a change and is indicative of what we can expect from here on out."

"Sure, Mr. Morton, you can count on me."

Morton looked at Stan. "And Paulson, you could copy a page out of Gunderson's book when it comes to preparing a proposal."

"I'll be sure to do that, sir."

Morton stood for a moment looking back and forth between Leif and Stan. Finally, he smacked his hand on the top of the cubical partition, "Well boys, got work to do, deals to seal. Can't spend all morning around the water cooler."

After Morton disappeared into the hall, Leif turned to Stan. "Hey, forget what I said before butt-wipe interrupted. I didn't mean it. It's just that some strange things have been happening, and I didn't think you'd be in the mood to hear about them."

"Like what?"

"You know I said my car died at the coffee shop."

"Leif, don't start."

"Hear me out. No matter what you think, it really did conk out that morning. I got the receipt for the tow and repairs." He pulled out his wallet, rummaging through a wad of receipts. "Here it is,' he said, holding it up for Stan to see. "After our conversation, my garage called and wanted to know if I wanted them to bring the car here or was I going to pick it up. Well, I was really confused at that point. I asked them who called them to get the car. They said it was me. They said I had met them at Hava Java and they picked up the car and dropped me off at work."

"Doesn't sound too strange to me." *He must still be high from the weekend.*

"It sure as hell does, cause I didn't call them, and I didn't meet them at Hava Java, but here's the receipt," Leif said. Stan rolled his eyes. "Wait, before you say anything," Leif continued, "that's not the only screwy thing that's gone down. Three days later, I get a text from Joe Aluka. You remember him from school? Anyway, he says what a great time we had at Jugs & Wings, and thanks me for picking up the tab." Leif paused. "Stan, with all the car business, I forgot all about it. I never met Joe for dinner, yet there was his text as big as life."

"Maybe he thought you were someone else."

"No he didn't, Stan. I checked my debit activity and there was a $147.00 charge from Jugs & Wings for that Wednesday."

"Somebody stole your PIN."

"No way! My card's in my wallet and all the other charges are legit, and that ain't all. Yesterday, I went to the dog races. When I got back my grass had been cut."

"A well intentioned neighbor."

"I don't think so. I ain't on very good terms with my neighbors. Anyway, I went over and knocked on Mrs. Ferrell's door. She's the biggest snoop in the neighborhood. If anyone would know who did it, it would be her. When I asked the old bag

124

if she saw who cut my grass, she just laughed and said I shouldn't try to play tricks on an old woman. She said it was me or my twin brother and it was about time I got around to mowing. Stan, I ain't got a twin brother. And there's other things too, like dishes being done and clothes washed and folded when I know I ain't done neither in weeks."

Stan's frustration boiled over. "If your laundry has mysteriously been done, then why in the hell didn't you at least put on a clean shirt? Listen, it's not for me to make judgements, and I've tried to keep my mouth shut, but you make it hard when you pull this kind of crap. You look like you've been on a bender all weekend. You can't be racing to the bottom of the bottle all the time or shoving dope up your nose without some serious consequences. Can't you see you're losing it? Why do you think Miriam left you? Wasn't because she didn't like the curtains. The best thing in your life, and you drove her away. You live life like a college kid on spring break. Take that back, that's not fair to college kids. But you know what I mean. Everybody is tired of your bull. I'm the only friend you got left, and that's hanging by a thread!"

"So I guess if you weren't pissed before, you are now."

Stan glared at Leif. "Well I'm sure as hell getting that way. I gotta get back to my desk."

* * *

The next morning Stan arrived for work, early as usual. He was surprised to find Leif at his cubical. "What's up?" he asked. "You're in bright and early. Say, didn't mean for yesterday to go the way it did." Stan could immediately see Leif was clean shaven, eyes bright and clear. He had on a crisp clean shirt and to Stan's surprise, a tie.

"Good Morning Stan. How goes it with you this fine morning?" Leif's usual snarky grin was replaced by a simple smile.

"Going just fine. Like the tie. Is that a new look for you?"

"Dress for success, Stan. There's a fresh pot of coffee in the break room, and we have about 15 minutes before we hit the old grindstone. Want to grab a cup?" Leif asked.

What's he up to? "Sure if you're buying. " They walked to the breakroom. Stan fixed his coffee at the tiny kiosk then stepped aside for Leif. Stan was surprised to see he did not dump a quarter cup of sugar and three salted caramel mocha liquid creamer singles in his cup as was his usual practice. Instead, he added two packets of artificial sweetener and a dash of skim milk. "Changing things up?" Stan asked.

"You could say that. How is Linda?"

He hasn't asked about her since Miriam left. "She's fine, relaxing, catching up on her reading. Summer vacation is the school teacher's favorite time of year."

Their conversation continued until Leif said, "Well, the clock on the wall says it's time to go to work and earn some money." He got up, rinsed his cup and set it in the strainer. "Hey, it's supposed to be nice today. Would you like to try a food truck for lunch?"

"Sure, that would be nice for a change."

"Okay, see you then."

* * *

About noon, Stan shut down his computer and headed for Leif's cubicle. "You ready?" he asked, poking his head in the opening. Leif was hunched over his desk, head resting on folded arms. "Leif," he said, increasing his voice to the maximum office volume. Leif did not respond. Stan stepped forward , nudging his shoulder. He could see the grime of several day's wear around Leif's collar. *Strange. Could've sworn it was clean this morning.*

"Huh?" Leif mumbled, lifting his head from his arms. He rubbed his bleary eyes, then ran his fingers through his disheveled hair. "Can't a fella get some sleep around here?"

Is that beard stubble? Geez, what's happened since this morning? "Hate to spoil your beauty sleep. It's lunchtime, pal."

"Where we going?"

"Lunch truck. Don't you remember?"

"I hate lunch trucks. Can't we go somewhere with air conditioning?"

"No, it was your suggestion in the first place, and I have been thinking about it all morning. Besides, it's nice outside. Come on, I'm sure we can find you something suitably greasy resting on a bed of fries."

"Well, if that's the case, I'm in."

They made their way down to the lobby and out through the big glass doors into the midday sunlight. Leif immediately put his hand to his forehead to shade his eyes. "Damn, I forgot my sunglasses," he griped. "Gotta go back in and get' em. You go on and get us a place in line. I'll catch up." He turned and disappeared into the building.

Stan was almost to the order window when Leif caught up. "What are you having?" he asked.

"I think I'm in the mood for a turkey and avocado wrap with some iced green tea," said Leif.

"What? No Philly cheesesteak and a slurpy?"

"Your body is a temple, Stan."

Stan looked at Leif. Somehow, the shirt that had looked so grimy in the fluorescent office light now appeared brand new. His face had no sign of beard stubble and his eyes were bright and clear. *Wait a minute!* "Say, I thought you went back to get your sunglasses."

"What and miss this beautiful day?" Leif pointed past Stan's shoulder to the attendant, "I think she is ready for us to order. We better not hold up the line." They got their orders and found a place to eat. As they unwrapped their sandwiches, Leif picked up the conversation. "Stan, you know the divorce papers have not gone through yet."

"Yeah."

"Well Miriam and I have been talking and she is willing to try a reconciliation."

"That's great news: that is, if you are ready to take that step."

"Of course I'm ready."

"Leif, I don't mean to go ugly on you, but you gotta know it's your turd-brained behavior that drove Miriam away, and if you haven't changed your ways, this reconciliation won't work. Granted, there's been times lately I think you've changed, but then there're other times when I can't see you've changed a bit. I don't mind telling you, it's hard being your friend, putting up with all the crap you dish out. It's frustrating not knowing what to expect next, watching you burn your candle at both ends. I can't imagine what it was like for Miriam. Don't put her through that again."

"You are absolutely right, and I am sorry for the way I have behaved. I assure you there is no need to worry about Miriam in the future."

"Well, know this. If you haven't changed or you hurt Miriam again, that cuts it for me."

"Understood."

They continued to eat in silence until Stan had almost finished his sandwich. His mobile chirped, signaling a message. He swiped across the screen. *What the hell?* It was from Leif .

'Is the other me there?'

Stan looked at Leif who was sipping the last of his tea. They had been together at least half an hour and Stan had not seen Leif use his phone. Stan keyed a reply,

'What's going on?'

and touched the send icon. In a few moments, his phone chirped again.

'Ditch him, MM @ drugstore'

Stan looked up from his phone. Leif was carefully folding up his empty sandwich wrapper.

"Time to get back," Leif said.

"We've got a few more minutes left before we gotta go back, why not enjoy the day?"

"I have a proposal I am anxious to finish today and I think a few minutes extra will just do the trick."

"Well, okay," said Stan. "If that be the case, I think I'll stop by the drugstore on the way back. There's something I need to do. Ready?" They walked together in idle conversation until they reached the drugstore on the corner across from their building. "Here's where I jump off. Catch you later." He slipped in the door and watched Leif until he stopped at the corner with the rest of the pedestrians. He nearly fell to the floor when he heard Leif's voice from behind.

"Can you still see the other me?"

Stan whirled around to find Leif stepping out from behind the cosmetics display. *I must be losing my mind.* In the fluorescent lighting of the store, this Leif's face looked ashen, hair unkempt and eyes bleary, not at all like the Leif he had just shared lunch with.

129

"Don't look at me," he said. "Make sure you keep your eyes on the other me till he gets inside the office."

Stan looked back to the corner. The other Leif was still standing there. The light changed and he crossed the street with the rest of the pedestrians. Stan watched until he went inside their building. "What the hell is going on?"

"I got a theory, but this ain't the place to discuss it. Do this. Wait a minute or two to let the other me get to my desk. Then call, not on my cell phone, but on my desk phone and see who answers."

"This is absurd. I don't know what you are up to, but I have had it with you and your bull." Stan's frustration was welling up.

"Make that call, and if you don't get an answer, I'll never say another word."

Stan glared at Leif. "If this is some prank, I swear I'll beat the crap out of you right here."

"Make the call."

Stan dialed the office number. The receptionist answered. "Hi Jeannie. This is Stan Paulson. Ring me up to Leif Gunderson's desk, please and thank you."

"Sure Stan," said Jeannie. "I think he's there. I just saw him come in."

The phone rang twice before Leif's voice answered. "Hello, this is Leif Gunderson. How may I help you?" Stan, stunned at the familiar sound of Leif's voice, remained silent. "Hello, is anyone there?" asked Leif.

"Oh, sorry, this is Stan. I was just thinking, I didn't ask you if you needed me to pick up anything from the drugstore for you."

"How nice of you to ask. Now that you mention it, some breath mints would be nice. My sandwich had onion on it and I have a meeting with Mr. Morton this afternoon. Wintergreen, if they have it."

"You got it. I'll see you in a bit. Bye." He touched the red circle on the screen, ending the call.

"Well?" asked the Leif next to him.

"I don't understand."

"Like I said, I got a theory, but this ain't the place to tell you. Besides, you probably feel like you got to get back to work. Me, I'm planning an afternoon of leisure. Meet me at Scalawags after you're done at work and I'll fill you in."

"Do we have to meet at a strip joint? You know Linda doesn't like me meeting you at places like that."

"You can go somewhere else, but if you want to find out what's going on, be there." Leif slapped Stan on the shoulder as he walked out the door heading away from their office.

Stan watched until he reached the end of the street and turned the corner. He contemplated what had just happened. *Nothing to do but play it out and meet him after work. How'd I ever get caught up in this mess?* Stan purchased a roll of breath mints and returned to the office.

Leif was busy typing away on his keyboard when Stan approached. "Here's your mints," Stan said, dropping the roll on the desk. "Wintergreen, as requested."

"Thanks. I appreciate you thinking of me." Leif looked up from his work.

Clear eyes, healthy complexion, hair all neat. This may be Leif, but sure as hell he isn't the Leif I just left at the drugstore. "Not a problem," said Stan. The afternoon slowly crept along. Stan found it hard to concentrate on work. His mind wandered. Finally, quitting time arrived and Stan shut down his computer. On one hand, he was anxious to get to Scalawags and on the other he was fearful of what he might learn.

* * *

Scalawags was a dark, dingy strip joint hovering on the edge of the downtown entertainment area. At 5:30 on a weekday afternoon, its parking lot was half full of cars with engines long cooled. Stan looked in vain for Leif's car. *Sonofabitch!* Uncomfortable sitting alone in the parking lot, he decided to go in. *15 minutes, then I'm gone.* He locked his car and went in. He stood just inside the door until his eyes adjusted to the dim light. The bar ran along the wall to his right. A runway emerged from the far wall ending as a circular stage in the center of the dark room. Customers encircled the stage waving bills at a nude dancer. Stan stepped forward, eyes straining to see the faces of the patrons. He jumped when a hand tapped his shoulder. He turned to see a frumpy waitress, breasts spilling out of an ill-fitting bikini top.

"He's over there." She pointed to a table along the far wall. Stan could see a figure sulking in the shadows. "Drink?"

"No thanks."

"There's a $15.00 cover if you don't buy a drink,"

"Club soda?"

"I'll bring it over."

Stan made his way around mostly empty tables until he was standing at the one the waitress had pointed out.

"Hey, you made it," said Leif. "Thought for a moment you were gonna blow me off. Have a seat. Did Jaylene get your order?" The table was littered with glasses. Stan could just hear Leif over the scratchy disco music that welled out of the speakers. He sat down just as Jaylene returned with his club soda and a drink for Leif. "My tab," Leif said.

Stan remained silent while Jaylene picked up the empty glasses. After she left he said, "Yes, and I almost didn't stay. Didn't see your car outside."

"I gave up driving." Leif took a sip of his drink. "The other me has the car. It's just easier to use rideshare when I need to go somewhere rather than try to work out who gets the wheels."

"From the number of glasses on the table, that probably makes good sense. Listen, I'm not here to pound you about how much booze you pour down your throat or how much dope you shove up your nose. You already know what I think about that. I want to know what is going on with this 'other me' crap. You said you had a theory."

Leif leaned forward. The shadows seemed to follow his face. "You might as well know, I ain't living at home anymore, either."

"Why?"

"Just too much trouble trying to share it with him."

"Where are you staying?"

"Got a room at the El Cambio across the way." Leif pointed over his shoulder with his thumb. "Works out real good. Most everything I need is within walking distance." Leif smirked, taking another sip from his drink. "And there's nothing to clean, bed made every day. A new bar of soap every Monday. While back at the ranch, the other me does all the work."

"How're you paying for all this? It's got to cost a lot to pay for a house and a rent a motel room at the same time, even if it is a room in that fleabag across the street."

"Didn't I tell you? I got another job. Just a few evenings a week at Quik Cash payday loans. Pays the bills."

"I take it you're off tonight."

"Oh no, my shift started a few minutes ago. Not to worry though. The other me is there verifying loan applications as we speak," Leif laughed. "You see the way I figure it, he's one of those dopplerbangers."

"You mean a doppelgänger."

"Yeah, that's what I said, a dopplerbanger. Somebody or something that looks just like me who's going around pretending to be me when I'm not there. But then, when I show up, 'poof', he's gone. Kinda like that D. B. Cooper guy, so I call him D. B. Gunder." Leif chortled. "That's short for dopplerbanger Gunderson."

Geez, he's gone completely mad. "Get hold of yourself. Do you even hear what you're saying? Do you have any idea how crazy it sounds?"

"You saw him, didn't you? Had lunch with him, didn't you? Heard him on the phone while you was standing right next to me, didn't you? Explain that."

Stan stared at the shadowy face across the table. It was Leif's face but it was different – sadder, distant. *How could it change so much since lunch? That face at lunch was friendly, confident, even hopeful.* Stan became aware of his heart beating inside his chest. He sucked in quick, shallow breaths and beads of sweat formed on his forehead. His muscles tightened. *By God, the sonofabitch might be right!* Stan took a moment to collect his wits. "Let's say for the sake of argument that what you say is correct." He hesitated, taking a deep breath, "Don't you think there is something very wrong or even worse, dangerous, with that?"

Leif tipped his glass up, draining the last of his drink. He held up his hand and called out for Jaylene. He slumped back in his chair, disappearing into the darkness. Behind Stan, the disco music stopped, followed by a smattering of claps and catcalls. A relative quiet of alcohol fueled babbling and glass clinking at the bar ensued.

"Jesus, Stan. Don't you get it? It don't matter if it is dangerous or not. All my life I've been just scraping along, working my ass off and getting nowhere. Never getting to live the good life, never getting my chance. The way I see it, this is my chance to live it up just once, even if only for a little while. What's wrong with that?"

"You call this the good life?" Stan asked, sweeping his arm around. "Drinking and drugging your life away with Jaylene to keep you company. Right now, the other Leif isn't waiting for the good life to fall into his lap. He's working at it. Doing the right things. Things you could be doing, if you would only give it a little effort. Do you even know this other Leif is looking to reconcile with Miriam? He's talked with her. He's going to see her. What happens then? Do you even care?"

"Well, that's my plan, Stanny boy. I'm gonna let that bastard do the heavy lifting. Let him work his little butt off until everybody thinks I've turned things around. Let him convince Miriam to give me another chance. Then all I got to do is just step back in. When the time is right, I'll just step back in and, 'poof', he's gone."

"You really think it's that simple?" asked Stan

"Why not?" Leif whined. "That's the way it's been working up to now, don't see any reason why it shouldn't work once all the hard work is done. I've been testing it out. Showing up late for work, leaving early. Not doing anything while I am there. No matter what I do or don't do, ol' D.B. covers. No one seems to know the difference. All my work gets done. In fact, I get compliments when I do show up. Back at the ranch, the bills get paid, the flower beds get weeded, the shrubs trimmed and I don't have to lift a finger. What's to worry about? All I need is for him to get me over the hump, then I can take it from there. You're just jealous that you ain't got a setup like this."

"That's all bull," Stan shot back. "I'm afraid this is going to go bad for you, very bad. Leif, two months ago, I would have said you were my best friend. Now, I don't know. As it stands, I think I like the other you better, if he even exists. And you aren't doing anything to change my opinion. You've got to come to your senses. You've got to step back in right now before this goes any further. You gotta promise me you will. Promise me?"

"I can step back in anytime I want. Believe me, it won't be a problem."

"Okay, prove it. Don't go back to the motel tonight. Go back to your house. Call me in the morning and show me you're right. Deal? If that works, I'll quit bugging you."

Leif smirked. "I tell you what. Not only will I step back in tonight, but I'll do it for a week. After that, you'll concede I'm right and shut up about all this."

"You got a deal. One week and I'll never say anything again. Call me when you get up tomorrow. I'll come over on the way to work just to make sure everything is on the level. I gotta go. Maybe you should do the same."

"The night is young, Stanny. I told you, I got everything covered."

"Okay. See you tomorrow morning?"

"With bells on."

Jaylene came up just as Stan turned to leave. He pulled out his wallet, dropping $20 on her tray. "My tab," he said, heading toward the door. As he left, Stan looked back at the table where he left Leif. He could barely make him out in the shadows.

* * *

Stan was still sound asleep the next morning when his cell phone chirped. He recognized Leif's number through waking eyes. He touched the screen. "Hey guy, you're up early. Must'a taken my advice and made an early night of it."

"Stan, "I need you to come get me." Leif's voice was barely audible.

"Speak up. I can't hear you."

136

"Stan you got to come right away." He sounded like he was in a hole.

"Are you at home?"

"At the motel, room C113. Hurry." The phone went dead.

Stan pulled off the highway into the El Cambio motel. He circled the parking lot until he came to room C113. He nosed his Prius into the narrow space between a beat up sedan and a rusting pickup truck. A maid's cart was standing by the open door of a room two doors down. Stan pounded on the door of C113. He waited for an answer. Hearing none, he pounded the door again. The maid emerged.

"Excuse me," Stan called to her, "have you serviced this room yet?"

The maid checked her clipboard, "Ain't nobody stayed in that room."

Stan looked at the number on the door. *Dammit, he said C113.* "You sure?"

"Yeah."

"Can you tell me what room Leif Gunderson is in? I got to see him."

"I wouldn't know. They'll know at the front desk. They won't tell you no room number though, but you can ask them to call your friend if he's staying here."

"Thanks," said Stan. He got back in his car and drove to the front entrance. He parked under the canopy and got out. Just as he approached the door, a familiar face appeared on the other side of the glass. *Leif! What the hell?* Stan stopped dead in his tracks.

Leif pushed the door open and stepped outside. "Stan, what a surprise to see you here. Meeting someone?"

"Uh, ye-yeah," he stammered. "And you?"

"Me? No, just settling accounts, making amends, letting things go." He looked into Stan's eyes. "That guy you came to see is gone."

"Gone? What happened?"

"I guess you could say he turned over a new leaf. No matter, I am here. Say, you want to grab a cup of coffee?"

Stan looked into the eyes of the smiling Leif. "Better not," he said, looking at his watch. "I'm late for work as it is. That means you're late, too."

Leif smiled. "Not really, You see I scheduled this vacation day a month ago." He put his arm around Stan's shoulder. "And do not worry about being late for work. We have you covered. Now, what about that cup of coffee?"

A SCALE-FREE CORRELATION

"Want me to bring you a piece?" Jay asked Robin. She was too engaged with her smartphone to answer. He shrugged and got out of the booth and walked over to the buffet line. He grabbed a green melamine plate and eyed the remnants of pizzas resting under red heat lamps on wobbly aluminum pans. It was 2:30 pm - the lunchtime crowd was long gone and the selections reflected that.

He could hear noise in the kitchen and ducked down to look. Five employees in red El Condor Pizza shirts huddled together around a small TV. "Hell-o-o," he said. No response. "Hey!" he called, upping the volume. This time, one turned his head and sauntered over. The rest followed closely behind.

"Yeah, man. What you need?" asked the employee wearing a condor wing name tag. "Woody" had been scrawled across it in purple marker.

"You the pizza chef, Woody?" Jay asked.

"Yeah, I guess you could call me that."

"Woody, let me ask you this. Got any pepperoni coming out?"

Woody stepped back and eyed the ovens. "Ahhh, that would be a no."

"Got anything coming out?"

"Just put a sausage and bacon in the oven?"

"That'll do."

"Sorry, that's for a carryout."

"And that's it?" Jay asked.

Woody looked down the buffet line. "Got a nice banana pepper and mushroom down there. That just came out about 10 minutes ago. And I see most of a big meat treat out there too. It's got pepperoni."

Jay looked around the dining room. Besides Robin and him, only one customer was in the store. A paunchy, balding man in sweats and a faded Road Runner t-shirt was seated in the back. He was strategically located directly in front of the big screen TV next to the wait station. Handy for refills. He was leaning back in his chair, head tilted up toward the screen. A stack of used plates showed he was done with his lunch. There wasn't going to be any peperoni going in the oven anytime soon.

"Thanks."

He took a piece of the big meat treat and returned to the booth, plopping down across from Robin. Over her shoulder, the TV displayed the news. The sound was muted, but he could just make out the closed caption to follow what was in the video footage. The scene cut away to what looked like a mall.

"You gotta see this," Robin squeaked pushing her phone in front of his face, almost knocking the pizza out of his hand. "Some kind of flash mob at a mall in the Philippines has gone completely cray-cray."

He pushed her hand to the side and pointed toward the big screen. "Yeah, I see it right there." Robin pulled her earbuds out and turned to see a low def security cam video playing on the screen. It showed a mob of people running clockwise in unison around the central rotunda of a huge mall. Suddenly, they changed direction, spiraling counterclockwise. All the while, more people flooded in from the side corridors. Then, the swarm compacted in the very center only to immediately flow out of the camera's view. The video loop started again. Wishing the sound was on, he squinted to read the closed-caption text floating over the screen.

A spokesperson for the Philippine National Police has released the following statement:
-The Director General has confirmed that a large number of people occupied the SM City North EDSA Shopping Mall In Metro Manila, Philippines this morning before escaping.-
Authorities can neither confirm or deny that when police arrived, the Mall was empty.

"See! Cray-cray," she reiterated.

"Probably some Guinness World Record stunt or something like that," Jay said, hoping to extend the conversation. Robin, however, had already reinserted her earbuds and returned to her smart phone. He chewed on his lukewarm pizza. It turned into a wad of dough in his mouth. He grabbed his tumbler and took a sip through the straw only to be met with a mouth full of air. The server was nowhere to be seen. Either she was still in the kitchen with Woody and the others or had gone outside to burn one. He yanked off the lid, using a greasy finger to scoop some crushed ice into his mouth.

"Ooh," Robin said, "More cray-cray."

Jay looked at the big screen. A new loop was playing. A woman was standing in a vineyard. The camera closed in on the vines which had been stripped of their grapes.

A spokesperson for the Livermore Valley Vintners Association has released the following statement:
A swarm of people described as numbering in the hundreds descended on this Green Heron winery early this morning in the Livermore Valley, devouring the entire crop.

The owner states that it appeared to be a coordinated effort because the invaders appeared to move in unison.

The scene switched to an aerial shot showing a huge group of people in the vineyard. As a farm truck approached, the crowd moved in mass to another section of the vineyard. Their movement reminded Jay of the way birds fly to their roosts in the Fall.

>>Whenever we approached, they all turned away, sweeping around in a great arc only to comeback from another angle.
We chased them all morning, but they kept coming back until the whole crop was gone.<<

"Mucho cray-cray," said Robin, looking back at her phone.

Jay poked the straw down through the crushed ice in a vain attempt to find any soda lingering in the bottom of his tumbler. Just then, the five El Condor Pizza employees filtered out from the kitchen and headed for the front door. Jay tried to signal the server, but in typical fashion, she walked out without acknowledging his waving hand. He turned to Robin.

"Did you see that? The whole damn bunch just walked outside. I don't see how this place stays in business." Robin continued staring at her smart phone, oblivious to Jay. "You're no better," he said. "Be careful or they might hire you. You'd fit right in."

The Road Runner guy got up from his table and walked to the front of the store. He paused at the front window. Then he left. The glare of the sunlight prevented Jay from seeing what he was watching. "Did you see that?" Jay asked. His question fell on deaf ears. "I think that guy just ducked out on his bill. Maybe I'll do the same thing. They deserve it for the way they treat their customers." Robin continued staring at her smart phone.

Jay's eyes searched the wait station. Just as he figured, the pitcher of soda the server used for refills was sitting there. It was at least half full. He grabbed his tumbler. He was going to ask Robin if she wanted a refill, but seeing she was locked onto her device, he decided to save his breath and get a refill for himself.

The remote for the TV was there. Jay looked around to confirm that he and Robin were the only people in the restaurant. "Why not?" he murmured, punching the mute button. The TV's speakers came to life.

> *"... to stay indoors as reports continue to come in. Again, it has been established that people have been spontaneously gathering in groups and committing acts of vandalism. Widespread investigation of these outbreaks has indicated that these swarms of people are roaming about, seeking food which they devour before moving along. Although no violent acts have been reported, people are cautioned to stay inside... "*

Robin looked up from her smart phone. "Wowie zowie," she shouted. "Just got a tweet from Sora. She says something big is happening over at Paloma High. See if you can get local 7 on the TV." Jay punched it up on the remote. A soap opera appeared on the screen.

"Nothing there," he said.

"Try local 5."

He pressed the down selector twice. Brant Brambling's face appeared. "Got something," Jay said, cranking up the volume.

"...able to give the public is this quote from Gadwall Police Chief King Eider, who is quoted as saying, 'Tell the people, for God's sake to get off the streets! Tell them to go home and lock their windows and doors up tight! We don't know what kind of food-happy characters we have here!'

If you have just joined Channel 5 News Live, we have breaking news. Earlier today, havoc broke out at Paloma High School. During a school assembly, reports say the entire student body, faculty, and school staff left the building and marched to the Gadwall Mall where they roamed around the building, twisting and turning and constantly changing direction before entering the building. Once inside, they continued to march around in what only can be described as a weird undulating pattern before swarming into the food court where they devoured everything in sight. Now to a live report from Anhinga Finch, who is outside the Gadwall Mall. Over to you Anhinga. . ."

The scene switched from the Channel 5 News Live studio to a bluff overlooking the Gadwall Mall parking lot. A young woman in a navy business suit stood center frame with one finger to her left ear and a microphone in her right hand. Her head was turned toward the scene behind her. People poured out of the main entrance to the Mall. The crowd whirled through the parking lot, drawing together to sift between the cars, then wildly swelling to fill the lanes. Sometimes they doubled back on themselves, reversing their direction, ever twisting, ever pulsating, but always in unison, not a single person moved contrary to the group's constantly changing direction.

"I know her!" Robin laughed. "Her real name isn't Anhinga Finch, it's Guadalupe Murrelet. She was the dumbest twit in our class. Hope they don't expect any profound insight from her."

"So, now you want to talk," said Jay. The TV continued to show Anhinga staring at the crowd now coursing through the Mall parking lot. Brambling's voice came over the speakers.

> ". . . Anhinga, can you hear us? What can you
> see?"

Anhinga turned to look into the camera, then turned back.

> ". . . Anhinga?"

She dropped the microphone and raced down the hill to join the crowd. The picture blinked back to the Channel 5 News Live studio, showing a bewildered Brant Brambling.

> ". . . Well it looks like we are having some
> technical difficulties with our remote transmission.
> We will now pause for a commercial message."

Jay flipped through the channels for a while to see what else was happening. Every channel carried similar reports of outbreaks of the unexplainable phenomena. Animal TV was showing clips of starling murmurations, comparing them to the swarms of people now being reported in every part of the world.

Jay watched the video in wonder as a flock of thousands of starlings flew together in a whirling, ever-changing pattern. They seemed connected to one another, able to twist and turn and change direction at a moment's notice. Each movement of a single starling reinforced the actions of the others, leading to and building on a spontaneous, though unified, cohesive activity.

"Robin, are you seeing this?" he asked. No response. He turned his head to look at her. She had been standing at his side watching but now had drifted to the front of the store. She was reaching for the door.

"Robin, stop," Jay yelled. "They said to stay inside."

"But they're coming," she said. "Can't you hear it, can't you feel it?" She opened the door, stepping into the sunlight.

"Robin! No!" Jay shouted, running to the front of the restaurant. The door had closed by the time he got there. He peered out the window. An endless flow of people passed. There was no leader, its fluid movement driven collectively, totally cohesive and indivisible. He could see Robin lingering for an instant at the edge before being swept up in the current. He watched as she moved along and was absorbed.

He continued to watch, mesmerized by the movement. As he did, he began to feel a rhythm, like a murmur deep within his being. It grew stronger, calling him. His hand waivered on the door until the murmur filled him and he could no longer hold back. Flinging the door open, he stepped into the sunlight.

Jay moved along in complete harmony with his flock mates until they reached Bobolink Park. There, the entire flock settled for a rest under the trees. After a while, the flock stirred and started moving once again. Although no one said anything, he knew they were headed to the farmer's market to eat before they headed south for the winter.

THE KILL[6]

The Depression was as hard on the residents of Potter City as it was anywhere in the country. All over, people struggled to survive in the midst of the worst economic crisis anyone living could remember.

Alphonse Perkins sat stiffly against the broad tree trunk. The afternoon light filtered through the leafless hemlock forest. This hunt in the bleak, unforgiving, Vermont winter had taken its toll. The chilling grayness, dulled by alcohol, blurred the boundary between the real and the imagined. He wasn't even sure how long he had been in the woods. Was it three days? Four? Why had Louis left? Alphonse would have gone home days ago had he not so desperately needed some money. So, he had continued shuffling through the forest in search of some meat while he swilled down cheap whisky to stave off the cold.

The carcass hung upside down from an overhanging limb. The blood flow had slowed to the occasional drip which fell into a congealing, crimson pool on the forest floor. He felt as lifeless as the lump of flesh before him. He had made the kill in the late morning. Bleeding would reduce the weight he had to carry out of the woods. Forest debris clung to his dress Wellingtons, and blood stained his herringbone tweed topcoat. These clothes were not particularly suited for hunting; but, times were tough, and Potter City's haberdasher of fine men's furnishings could ill afford regular hunting attire. He drained the last of the whisky and let the bottle fall carelessly at his feet.

He reckoned the carcass weighed about 170 pounds and should fetch a good price from Sgozzare. He detested dealing

---

[6] The Kill appeared on line in Flash Fiction Magazine, 6/27/2017.

with the butcher; but, in order to make ends meet, he had to make some concessions. As a young man, he had often hunted with his father and brother Louis, but had given it up as crass and beneath his position. After all, the man who dressed the elite of Potter City was above the vulgar pursuits of the common mill worker. None-the-less, it was Louis who had struck on the idea of supplying fresh meat to Sgozzare. Alphonse detested it. Still, they had been able to earn a few dollars in a time when dollars were scarce. Now, though it had been a strained partnership, he wondered why Louis wasn't beside him to help.

Alphonse carefully untied the carcass and fashioned a sling to drag it out of the forest. He calculated that he should reach his Model T just before sunset. By the time he reached Potter City, it would be dark and few, if any, would be able to see him pull around to the rear of Sgozzare's with his prize strapped to the hood.

Frost formed on his mustache as he labored to make his way through the thick forest. His feet were stiff and aching from hours walking through snow and the freezing air assaulted his lungs. Fresh daylight was waning as he reached the road where his car was parked. He slumped for a moment on the running board. The cadaver was barely recognizable in the dimming light without its beating heart to give it living structure and purpose. Just meat, he thought, just meat.

Summing all his remaining strength, Alphonse wrestled the limp body up on the hood of his car. He slumped once again on the running board, sucking in more freezing air, stinging his depleted lungs. He got up and stumbled to the trunk to retrieve some rope to lash his ghoulish hood ornament down for the trip back to Potter City. After his numb fingers tied the last knot, he started the car and reached under the seat for a pint of whisky. A long pull from Van Winkles' Special Reserve served to warm his cold blood.

The last light of day had drained out of the sky and the deep rose of the western horizon gave way to pitch black overhead as Alphonse weaved through the narrow alley and stopped at the rear of the butcher shop. He tipped the half pint straight up, sucking the last drops of liquor from its narrow mouth. Stepping from the car, he stumbled to the rear door of the dreary brick building. The odor of rotting meat stuffed into rusting garbage cans filled his nostrils as he beat at the door. There was no response. He flung the empty bottle down the alley shattering it on the rough cobblestones, the shards joining the other refuse. Another tattoo of pounding was rewarded with the sudden appearance of a dim light above the door.

The angry voice of Sgozzare demanded to know who was breaking his door down at such an hour. Alphonse explained that he had come with fresh meat. The butcher responded by releasing the latch on the door. He stared momentarily into his unwanted guest's bleary eyes and instructed him to bring it in. Then he turned away saying he would return once he put on his apron. Alphonse stumbled back to the car and untied his quarry.

Hefting it on his shoulder, he bulled through the door and laid the carcass on the large, cut-gouged block just inside door and flopped himself on a small three legged stool in the corner. He could see little in the dark room lit only by the light that seeped in from the small bulb over the rear door. He could hear Sgozzare babbling to his wife in Italian from the other room. His eyes grew heavy as he waited for the butcher to return.

The sudden flash as Sgozzare turned on the lights blinded Alphonse's eyes. He heard the butcher gasp and his wife scream. As he struggled to his feet and his eyes cleared and focused, he gasped at the sight of his brother, Louis, lying on the butcher's block before him.

OSTATNI BILET

Lonelle Turner scratched Pogo behind the ears as he closed his eyes and dreamed of a childhood Sunday afternoon, sitting on his Grandma's porch, but with a storm cloud looming just beyond the creek bank. All the family had just come from church, laying fixings out on the big table. They feasted on fried chicken, ham sandwiches, dressed eggs, and the like. While they ate, the children would sit quietly and listen to the grown-ups talk. The boys wore blue serge trousers with white starched shirts, buttoned at the neck. The girls wore blue or pink dresses. Beads of sweat would roll down Lonelle's smooth brown face.

After dinner, the mothers cleaned up the kitchen while talking of husbands and children, shopping and cooking. The fathers sat out back drinking beer and discussing work, fishing and politics, in no particular order. The children got to sit on the porch with Grandma. Grandpa and his sons had built it on the side of the house. They had cut a big double door in the living room wall. It was screened on three sides and shaded by large oak trees. Lonelle knew as long as he stayed on the porch, he'd be safe from the storm.

The highlight of the afternoon was tea with Grandma. She would set out her favorite green glass tumblers and fill them with tea and ice. Then she would bring out a large silver tray heaped with fancy cookies from the bakery.

Her old wicker rocker creaked as the runners moved back and forth on the grey plank flooring. The grandchildren drew their chairs around, each vying to secure a spot next to her. But no matter where they sat, she talked with each in turn as if he or she was the only person there. No matter what was told her, she treated it with the utmost attention, interjecting her own commentary and occasionally recounting a similar experience from her childhood as well as a few stories about her own children. She possessed an uncanny knowledge of every mischief and forgotten chore, but never failed to praise an accomplishment or cite a good deed. As long as she talked, the storm cloud stayed beyond the creek.

Lonelle had looked forward to these afternoons as much as he had dreaded going home in the evening. He was five when his real father died at the Battle of the Bulge in late 1944. His brother, Vonelle, was four. After General Eisenhower, faced with Hitler's advancing army on the Western Front, temporarily desegregated the army, Lonelle's father was among the 2000 black soldiers, normally relegated to service units, who volunteered to join the fight. His mother had not remarried, but 'Uncle' Ray had moved in. Ray spent his Sunday afternoons drinking sloe gin and brooding. By the time they got back to the house, he was either ready to sleep it off or in a beatin' mood. Sadly, it was too often the latter.

Lonelle woke from his nap. He looked out the window of his kitchen, watching the summer afternoon drift by. Is that a storm cloud coming? He blinked his eyes and looked again. Naw, must'a been a dream. Condensation rolled down the sides of his tall, green iced tea glass – one of Grandma's glasses. Each time he took a sip, he carefully placed the glass back down in the ring of water that had collected on the big table. Pogo sat next to him, wet nose pressed against his thigh to remind Lonelle he was there. Occasionally, the yellowed curtains drifted inward on the breeze as if the old house was taking a deep breath, only to press them flat against the rusted screens as it exhaled. The fragrance of honeysuckle complemented the pleasant taste of his freshly brewed sweet tea - his Grandma's recipe. He soaked in the activity of the old neighborhood. Children gathered together in small clumps up and down the street. Dogs barked. Old women tugged at weeds in their flower gardens. Delivery and service men made their rounds. Young mothers sat on porches with their babies and talked and laughed and dreamed of better lives.

Pogo yipped at movement in the side yard, drawing Lonelle's attention back to the present. "What's that you see out there?" Lonelle asked. Pogo yipped again. "That's what I thought you'd say." He peered at the narrow gravel alley which ran alongside his property. An old shed leaned precariously against rotting fence posts next to a narrow gate that was secured with a rusty chain and padlock. He watched as a young boy crawled between the fence planks. The child quickly reconnoitered the shed and tugged desperately at its locked door. Dropping to one knee, he proceeded to prise the door open enough at the bottom to squeeze in.

Damn kids, always getting where they ain't supposed to be. Lonelle got up to go shoo the young intruder off, but before he got to the door, he spied a man slink up the alley and stop at the gate. *Now what's goin' on?* Pogo let out a low growl. Lonelle could hear the man shouting, but could not make out what he said. The man shook the gate furiously, then climbed over the fence and began to beat on the door of the shed. *That done it!* Lonelle opened the cupboard and retrieved his gun. He snatched up his keys, dropping them in his pocket along with the gun.

"You stay here," he said to the dog as he pushed through the screen door. "Can't have two old fools out there." He worked his way over the gravel path to the shed. The braces on his legs made for a slow and difficult journey. The man continued to beat the door with unrestrained ferocity. Lonelle had seen this kind of rage before and it made his heart pound. His own anger welled up into a steely resolve. "See here, what you think you're doing. This here is private property," he called out.

Startled, the man wheeled around and shouted back, "None of your goddamned business, old man." His eyes burned with hatred.

"It's my business when you're trespassin' on my property. Now you need to git." Lonelle pointed to the street with his cane.

"I'm lookin' for Chigger," the man said defiantly. "I saw him come down this alley, and I think he is hidin' in this shed."

"Who's that?"

"My girlfriend's kid. She's a Chicano and her baby's daddy's a . . ." the man leaned forward sneering at Lonelle, ". . . well, . . you can guess." He was close enough that Lonelle, could smell stale tobacco, body odor, and alcohol. It was the beatin' smell. Anger welled up in Lonelle. His hand clenched the revolver tightly. There ain't gonna be no beatin' today.

"Ain't no kid here, and I told you to git!" Lonelle declared.

"I ain't leaving 'till I'm sure."

"I told you there ain't no kid here," Lonelle said pulling the revolver from his pocket, "and this here is telling you to git."

The man looked at the revolver and laughed. "Boy, what makes you think you're going to do any damage with that .22?"

Lonelle's cheeks burned with anger. "Nothin'. This here will only make a little hole. Prob'ly feel just like a bee sting. Jus' a little hole in your belly. That slug will roll 'round in there a little. I bet it don't even come back out. Then, some kid, fresh out of med school, will finish the job down at the County hospital. I'll leave it to him to open you up an' look 'round 'fer it. He'll gut you like a fish, huntin' that little old chunk o' lead, and then close you up with a thousand stitches. Hell, I'll bet you'll be eatin' your meals through a tube for six months."

The man glared at the gun through bleary eyes. He pointed a finger at Lonelle, but said nothing. Backing off, he scrambled over the fence. Once on the other side, he gave Lonelle the finger, then stumbled off. Lonelle returned the revolver to his pocket with a trembling hand. Good thing it wadn't loaded or I'd a shot that bastard.

Jorge huddled in the corner of the shed. The heated conversation outside had died out and all was quiet again. Still, he was terrified. A slit of sunlight knifed through the closed shutters, glinting off the swirling dust. It was cloyingly hot in the still air of the shed. Wanting to take in a deep breath to still his beating heart, but afraid any noise would give him away, he struggled to control his breath,. He looked around. Old garden tools leaned against the opposite wall. A table piled with boxes, cans and tools covered with the detritus from years of non-use stood at the rear. His side of the shed was crammed with boxes.

A sliver of light fell across a tear in the cardboard box to his right. Through the hole, Jorge could see something shiny. Intrigued, he probed the hole with a shaking finger. The weathered cardboard crumbled away. Inside, Jorge could see something black with wheels. It gleamed in the sliver of light. There was not a speck of dust on it. Drawn to it, he reached his small hand through the crumbling opening and retrieved the object. He examined it in the sparse light. It was a small train engine, an old steamer, like the ones he had studied in school. It was heavy in his hand. He could see more shining objects in the box and was about to reach in for another when the shed door creaked open, letting a narrow slab of light slice through the darkness.

"Alright, come out here," came a voice from the opening, "before I have to come in and get ya'."

Jorge didn't move.

"I know you're in there, so you might as well come out. That fella is gone, you don't have to worry 'bout him, but if you don't come out, you'll have to worry about me. So come on out." Jorge remained motionless. Lonelle leaned in the opening, eyes tracing the inner perimeter of the shed until they fell on the boxes. There, he spied a small hand holding the engine. He pushed the door open, allowing sunlight to flood into the shed. The features of the young boy emerged from the darkness. "There you are. What do you think you're doin' in here, goin' through a person's private things? Ain't you got no respect? Get over here, right now," Lonelle barked, rapping his cane on the floor in front of him.

Jorge could make out the old man's face, creased with lines, topped with thinning white hair. Wire rim glasses perched on a thin nose. He held a wooden cane in his left hand and he held his right over his eyes as if he were looking far off to some distant horizon. Jorge got to his feet and stepped from the boxes before he realized he still had the engine clutched tightly in his hand. He quickly concealed it behind his back hoping it had not been seen. He avoided looking into the old man's eyes. Wanting to bolt for the door, he looked about for a clear way to escape.

"What's your name, young man?" Lonelle asked in a calm voice. Jorge remained silent. "Look here, I ain't gonna do nothin' to you, and you can go if you've a mind to, but I think the least you could do is tell me your name. After all, this is my shed and them are my boxes you been foolin' with." Lonelle paused. "Least ways, if I was you, I'd let that fella, who was makin' all that ruckus, move on a bit before I got back on the street. Anyways it's too damn hot in this old shed, so why don't you tell me who you are so's I can ask you to come sit on the porch and have somethin' cold to drink."

"Jorge," came the barely audible reply.

"D'you say Hooray?"

"Jorge."

"How you spell that?"

"J. . .O. . .R. . .G. . .E"

"Well, Hor-Hay, why don't you come up to the house and have somethin' cold to drink with me whilst we let trouble be on its way? What do you say?"

"OK."

"Good. My name is Lonelle Turner, but you can call me Mr. Turner for short. And by the way, what's that you got behind your back?"

"Honest, mister, I was just looking at it. I wasn't gonna take it," Jorge pleaded, holding the engine out toward Lonelle. Jorge had to strain to hold the heavy toy at arm's length while the old man looked at him.

"I suppose if you don't take it outta the shed, then it jus' lookin'," Lonelle said, as he took the engine from the boy's trembling hand. "Now, go along to the house while I close up here."

Jorge sat on the porch steps watching the old man come slowly up the path, tapping his cane on gravel with each step. The engine, still clutched tightly in his hand, glinted in the hot afternoon sun. Lonelle did not say anything as he walked up the creaking porch steps past the boy. Setting the engine on the small white table sitting between two old wicker rockers, he told Jorge to have a seat, then disappeared through the screen door. Jorge hopped up into one of the rockers and studied the engine. Soon

Lonelle appeared at the door with a tray on which sat two green glasses and a matching pitcher filled with sweet tea.

"Come on out here," he called while holding the screen door open with his hip, "we got a guest." Jorge looked toward the open door. Pogo poked his head out and sniffed the air. "Come on, I ain't got all day. This here is Hor-Hay. Hor-Hay, this here is Pogo." The dog stepped around Lonelle onto the porch and approached Jorge with a hop, step, step.

"Why's he only got three legs?" asked Jorge. Pogo pushed his graying muzzle into the boy's leg looking for a pat on the head which he promptly received.

"He's smarter than the rest of them dogs. Only needs three to get around where the rest needs four," Lonelle said, placing the tray on the table. He dug a hand in his pocket and drew out a dog biscuit. "Here you go, give him this and he'll leave us be". Jorge took the biscuit and held it out for the eagerly awaiting dog. Pogo curled up next to Jorge's rocker content to chew on his treat.

Before Lonelle took the other rocker, he poured the sweet concoction into the glasses. He sat down and joined Jorge who was staring intently at the gleaming black steamer. After a long sip of tea, he pointed at the engine, "Got that from old Mr. K. He lived down on Branch Road. That's all gone now. Urban renewal tore down all them houses. Said they was gonna build some new ones, but they never did. Just an excuse to get rid of folks they didn't want around. Anyways, I did odd jobs for him when I was a kid. Just a little older than you. You know, pull weeds, rake leaves, paint the fence. I could get around better in these old braces back then, but it was still real hard. I guess kids don't do that much these days. Too busy playin' video games and list'nin' to their I-things. Back then, money was hard to come by and I was happy to have the work." Lonelle paused and took a long sip of tea. Jorge sat quietly in the rocker. "Go ahead and have some tea, it won't poison you. Anyways, he wadn't from around here, but had lived in town for a long time. Said he was from Poland. Said he had come here to escape from the Nazis. Sometimes, it was hard to understand him because he had such a thick accent, but he was good to work for and paid purdy good too."

"What's Natsies?" asked Jorge.

"They was real bad folk, like a black cloud blowin' in a storm of hatin' and killin'. Anyways, the last summer I worked for Mr. K., we spent a lot of time packin' his things up in boxes. He said he was goin' away. I asked him where. Said he was goin' to be with old friends. We went through his whole house 'cept for the basement. He said there was only a few things down there and he would take care of them hisself. That was the last time I saw him."

"What happened to him?"

"Don't rightly know. A few months later, a lawyer showed up at the door. He said a Mr. Kuglarz had died and left something for me in his will. I didn't know who this Mr. Kuglarz was. The lawyer handed me a letter. Once I read it, I figured out that Mr. Kuglarz was Mr. K. I was real sad to know he had passed. In the letter, Mr. K said one day, he hoped, I would find value in his gift. It was them boxes you found out there in the shed. The only things in them boxes was this here toy engine and a bunch of other train stuff. I didn't really know what to do with it, but I kept it all these years just the same."

Jorge looked suspiciously at the tea then took a tentative sip and smiled.

"You like that?" Lonelle asked. Jorge nodded in response. "You ever had sweet tea before?" Jorge shook his head. "Well I'll be, ain't never had no sweet tea. Well, when you finish that, you can have another." Jorge smiled.

"How's it work?" he asked.

"How's what work?"

"That," Jorge said pointing to the engine.

Lonelle picked up the train and brought it close to his glasses. He turned it over and around, carefully examining every nook and cranny. "Don't know. Never looked at it too close before. Been boxed up almost fifty years. Don't think it runs on 'lectric. I'm sure it don't run on steam," he chuckled. He brought the train close to his face, peering into the tiny cab. There he saw an assortment of brass gears filling the boiler compartment. Then he looked along the top of the boiler and spied a delicate keyhole concealed amid the fine detail that adorned the sleek engine. "Well, I'll be," he laughed, "I think you wind this thing up."

"Can we wind it up?" Jorge asked, leaning forward. He strained to see what the old man was pointing to.

"If I had the key, I would, but I don't, so's we can't.

"Can't we get the key?" Jorge pleaded.

"If I knew where it was, I'd get it in a heartbeat; but I don't, so's we can't. I 'speck it's out there in one of them boxes," he said, pointing toward the shed.

"Can't we go get it?"

"Not so fast. It's gettin' late, and I am all tired out from all the goin-ons we had 'round here this afternoon. No, it's too late to go diggin' in them boxes this evenin'. Mebbe if you come 'round tomorrow, we can take a look. Not that I'm promisin' nothin', but mebbe. Now, after you finish your tea, you best be gettin' home. I 'speck that fella - what's his name?"

"Bobby Ray."

"A two-name redneck, I should'a knowed!" Lonelle growled. "No matter. Most likely, this here Bobby Ray has forgot it all by now and your mom's prob'ly waiting on you for supper. Where 'bouts you live?"

Jorge pointed toward the housing project a couple of streets over. He sipped the last sweet liquid from the glass and hopped down from the rocker. Looking at the engine on the table and then at Lonelle he asked, "Tomorrow?"

"Mebbe."

Lonelle watched the child run along the gravel path and slip out through the fence. He poured the remaining tea in his glass and tossed another biscuit to Pogo. "Sure hope that child is gonna be OK. You think I should'a sent him packin' off like that?" Pogo looked up momentarily, then returned his attention to the biscuit. "That's what I thought you'd say. Still, can't help worryin'. I remember what it was like comin' home an' wonderin' what was gonna happen. Not knowin' if I was gonna get beat or if mama was gonna be cryin' 'cause of Vonnie. Naw, I sure hope Hor-Hay gonna be OK."

Lonelle sat on the porch, lolling between sleep and wakefulness while the sun dipped low in the sky. Images of roiling storm clouds filled his head. Winds carried his name, spoken by a voice he hadn't heard for many years. He felt a nudge on his leg, "I guess that means you're ready for supper?" Lonelle said to Pogo. The dog wagged his tale. "That's what I thought you'd say. Why don't we have somethin' real special tonight?" Pogo licked his chops. "Alright, weenies it is," Lonelle laughed.

He was just getting ready to settle into his easy chair and watch some TV when he remembered the engine. Best not leave that outside. He looked at Pogo. "Don't suppose you'd go get it for me, would you?" Pogo laid down next to the recliner as if he had not heard a thing. "Humph, I guess I jus' have to go get it myself, then." He hurried through the kitchen to the door. He turned on the porch light before stepping out. A single 40 watt bulb hung down from the peeling porch ceiling. It came to life, casting a warm glow over the porch area. The light glittered off the intricate brass fittings of the black engine. Lonelle was amazed how good the engine looked after all the years it had spent in the shed. It could have been new out of the box that night. He could see how it might spellbind a young boy. In the dim porch light, the engine almost glowed. For a moment, he gazed at it against the white surface of the table. He imagined the locomotive, full size, steaming out of snow covered steppes, approaching its destination, its shrill whistle shattering the brittle winter night's air. He picked the engine up gently and slipped back into the house.

He placed the engine on the stand by his recliner and sat down. He unfastened the leather straps of his leg braces and set them carefully aside. They were very old and heavy. He had forgotten how many times the leather straps had been replaced and how many times the hinges had been reworked. Every time they needed repairs, the technician tried to convince him to get new ones made of lightweight aluminum with Velcro straps, but he always refused. He pulled the lever on the side of his chair to raise the footrest. It felt good to lean back with his legs up, free of the braces. He reached over and picked up the engine. It had been a long and tiring day. He looked at the tiny keyhole in the top of the boiler. Gonna have to find that key. He turned off the lamp next to his chair and spent some time flipping through the channels on his television. The happenings of the day kept running through his head, sapping his interest, so he turned off the television and closed his eyes. He slipped in and out of restless sleep.

Lonelle woke to Pogo's soft whimper. He saw a young boy standing beside his chair. Not fully awake, he thought it was Jorge. "What are you doing here?" he stammered. "No, it can't be." He engaged the lever on the side of the recliner so he was sitting upright, then rubbed his eyes, hoping the vision was only the residue of a dream.

"Lonnie, wake up its Vonnie."

Lonelle closed his eyes expecting to wake up from the dream. He opened them again. The boy was still there. "Vonnie, that can't be you. You been dead a long, long time. I mus' be dreamin'." He looked at the figure in front of him. It sure looked like Vonnie. He was all muddy, clothes tattered. His left arm hung limp at his side.

"No you ain't dreamin' Lonnie, it's me. I thought you was dead. Thought I'd never see you again. I've tried to get back, but never could." He pointed to the engine Lonelle still clutched in his hands, "I see you got the engine. That mus' be it, why I's able to come back t'night. Thought you died that day at the creek. I wanted to tell Mama what happened."

"Mama's been dead a long time."

"I figured that might be the way it was, but when the chance come up to come back, I decided to give it a try. Anyways, I wanted to see you, too."

"No, this has got to be a dream. It was you that died at the creek that day. Don't you remember, we snuck off from Grandma's an' got to playin' up on them rocks high above the creek? We was wrasslin' 'round, when we tumbled over the edge. I landed on the rocks, and you must have tumbled into the water and got swept away and drowned. 'Least ways, that's what Ray said. I don't really remember anything. Ray said he saw the whole thing. He said he followed us up there to call us for supper and saw us wrasslin' and disappear over the bank. They say I almost died. Caved in my head on the rocks. I was out for two weeks. Couldn't walk for months. They never found you." Tears welled up in his eyes. "Vonnie, I'm sorry, I never meant no harm. I've missed you all these years. Never got to tell you I was sorry. Ray said it was my fault, said he told us not to go up there. Mama never was the same. She jus' couldn't stop cryin'. Then, she drunk herself to death. My fault, all my fault."

"Lonnie, it wasn't your fault."

"Yes, it was, Ray seen it all."

"Ray's a dirty liar. I hope he's dead and burnin' in hell. Didn't happen like that at all. I had gone up to the big walnut tree at the edge of the bluff above the creek behind Grandma's. Ray had told us to stay 'round the house, but I decided to sneak off. I was seein' how far I could throw walnuts across the creek when you come runnin' up to say Ray was huntin' for me, madder than hell. Ray must've seen you comin' across the field, 'cause he was right behind you, looming up like a big ol' storm cloud . Well, he grabbed me and started wailin' away. He was jus' beatin' an' beatin' me and it hurt real bad. I was cryin' and beggin' for him to stop, but he just kept beatin' on me like a hail storm. That was when you grabbed his arm. Why, I'll never forget the look in his eyes as he turned 'round and grabbed you 'round the throat. 'I'll kill you for that,' he said. Honest Lonnie, I was so scared and was hurtin' so bad, I couldn't do nothin'. I thought for sure he was going to kill you and I was going to be next, so I jumped. Just made it to the water, but it wadn't deep enough to keep me from breakin' my arm and putting a nasty cut on my head. I could hear you screamin' an' jus' as I looked up, I saw Ray hit you an' you stumbled back and fell over the side. God a' mighty, you hit the rocks like a sack o' taters. You didn't move or nothin'. By then, I was bein' drug down the creek. Honest, I thought you was dead. Ray was looking down from up top, so I ducked down and let the creek take me away.

"Lonnie, I can't stay no longer. My arm has started hurtin' real bad. Ain't hurt a bit since I left, but it sure hurts now. If I get a chance, I'll come back, mebbe tomorrow. There's more I got to tell ya'. But, I can't do it now. Got to go."

Lonelle reached out with a trembling hand to grasp his brother, but his fingers passed through the gauzy shape as if it were smoke. He watched his brother fade into the shadows beyond his chair. Just a dream. He drifted back to sleep only to continue dreaming uneasily of the cliff behind his Grandma's. In it, he and Vonnie careened endlessly through the air toward the rocky creek bed while Ray stood at the top and laughed.

Lonelle felt a warm sensation on his hand. He opened his eyes to find Pogo licking his fingers. "Dreamed I seen Vonnie last night," he said, stretching his arms out above his head. "Ain't done that in a long time." He was overcome with deep sadness. The dream had dredged up painful memories. The morning sunlight poured in through the windows. He went through the motions of his daily routine, but his thoughts were wandering in the past. Last night's dream upset him greatly. He had spent considerable time and energy blocking the painful memories of Vonnie's death and its tragic aftermath. Although his mother had never come out and said it, Lonelle was certain she blamed him for Vonnie's death. She only lived only a few years following the incident at the creek. Lonelle watched her withdraw into drink and depression until she died alone and heartbroken. He blamed himself for both Vonnie's death and her sad, slow demise. It was a terrible burden he bore silently and painfully.

Throughout the day, he kept watch for Jorge, wondering whether or not the child would return. He held mixed feelings about seeing the boy. On the one hand, he would be happy to have the opportunity to draw his thoughts away from the previous night's dream. On the other, he harbored resentment toward Jorge, justified or not, blaming him for the re-emergence of these dark memories. The sun drifted down the afternoon sky until it touched the tree tops. Lonelle, convinced the boy would not return, grabbed up the engine and started off to the shed. Out of sight, out of mind. Just put this damn thing back in the shed along with all them old memories.

He held the screen door open and called out, "Come on dog, let's go out to the shed." Pogo groaned as he got up from his spot under the big table. He wandered out on the porch and watched Lonelle drag along the gravel path to the shed. He sniffed the air, then slowly followed.

Lonelle propped the door wide open, hoping to allow some light and breeze into the dark, hot shed. He had nailed the shutters down some years ago and was not in the mood to try and pull nails in the heat of the day. Pogo, uninterested in the inner workings of the shed, plopped down in the tall grass and watched Lonelle disappear though the door. After his eyes adjusted, Lonelle examined the boxes and found the one with the hole from which Jorge had retrieved the engine. He couldn't figure how to place the engine back through the hole without tearing the whole side out of the box, so he carefully unstacked the boxes, setting them about on the dusty floor. Sweat trickled down his face. Finally, he reached the engine box and set it on the floor. Pulling a low stool from under the tool bench, he sat down and gingerly pulled the brittle cardboard flaps apart.

Inside he found the tender and caboose wrapped in old newspaper. Wiping the dust from his hands, he lifted them out and examined the crumbling newspaper pages. They were the Sunday comics. Above the faded panes of a Dick Tracy adventure, he found the date: November 18, 1956. Below Dick Tracy, Daisy Mae chased Li'l Abner and on the opposite page, Dagwood was in trouble again. Lonelle chuckled as he took time to read the old comics. After a while, he returned his attention to the bottom of the carton, where he found a model of a train station wrapped in cotton batting, which disintegrated as he pulled it away from the tiny building. It was complete in every detail. Lonelle marveled at the intricate and masterful craftsmanship of the object. Although the boxes, newspapers and cotton batting were badly deteriorated, the tender, caboose and the station appeared to be in pristine condition. They had not suffered the least bit from their long, forgotten stay in the shed.

The heat of the shed and the exertion of handling the boxes finally took their toll. He leaned back against wall, cradling the train station in his lap. He closed his eyes and took in a deep breath.

"Lonnie, wake up it's me."

Lonelle opened his eyes. His brother stood before him.

"Told ya' I'd come back. I got to tell ya' the rest of the story. You got to listen close. You got to believe. You understand?"

"Go away, you's jus' a dream come to punish me for what I done." Lonelle covered his eyes with trembling hands.

"No, Lonnie, this ain't no dream, I'm really here, jus' not here like regular folks, but here jus' the same."

"Go away, I said, leave me alone."

"Lonnie you got to listen, I ain't got much time an' I don't know if I'll be able to come back again, so you got to listen."

"No."

"But you got to listen. I got somethin' important to tell you. An' you got to believe it or it won't do you no good. I wanted to come for a long time, but I never could. Now you got the engine and I can come to you, but I can only do it for a little while an' time is running out. You got to believe me.

"I got to tell you what happened after I jumped in the creek. You see, I floated awhile until I got near the bridge. You know where the banks flatten out, just before it goes through Old Town. I crawled up on the bank an' hid under the bridge through the night and all the next mornin'. I started walkin' behind the old houses along Branch Road until I ended up at the backyard of a house with a big ol' apple, its limbs so loaded they was jus' about to break down. I was so hungry, I crawled through the fence and picked as many as I could stuff in my shirt. It was hard to do 'cause my arm hurt so bad. There was an old shed behind the house and I snuck in there and commenced to eatin' them apples. Wouldn't you know it, I hadn't hardly taken the first bite before the door flew open and this old man was standing there. I was awful scared, what with runnin' away and then bein' caught stealing apples and all. I thought for sure he was goin' to call the sheriff, but you know what? He said for me to come up to his house. I couldn't hardly understand him 'cause he had a foreign accent. When we got up to his house, he gave me some food. My arm was hurtin' real bad. He asked if he could take a look. God a' mighty, Lonnie, when I pulled up my sleeve, my arm was bent, right here." Vonnie held out his left arm and pointed to a spot just above the elbow. "He asked me what happened. I told him everythin' and begged him not to say nothin'. He sat there for a long time, jus' smoking his pipe.

"Finally, he said, 'You 'ave decision to make. You cannot go on like 'dis. Your arm it is broke and someting mus' be done. As I see it, you only 'ave two choices. One, I take you to doctor, in which case you will eventually 'ave to go back to the situation from which you run. Or two, you can take 'da train, in which case you will 'ave to leave everyting you know here.'

"Honest, I didn't know what he was talkin' 'bout, but I was ready to do anythin' rather than go back. So's I said I'd jus' as soon leave. Well, he led me down to the basement. Lonnie, you should a seen the layout he had down there. Had that train," he said, pointing to the engine, "an' a whole lot of other stuff set up jus' like a little town. Had houses, buildings and little people all about. It was sure somethin' to see. He told me to stand next to the engine, then he got out a small wooden box with funny writin' on it. He opened it up and took out a book.

"He said, 'What your name? I must record name of each passenger before issuing ticket.' I told him and he wrote it down. Then he reached in the box and pulled this out." Vonnie dug his hand into his pants pocket and drew out a stub of paper. "He said, 'You must 'ave ticket to ride train,' and handed me this." Vonnie held the stub up for Lonelle to see. It had a single word on it: BILET. Then the old man said, 'You mus' listen, very important, keep dis ticket with you always. Tak jest – take this.' I said OK.

"Next, he put a gold key in the top of the engine and commenced to windin' it up. Finally, he pushed the little bell on the engine and that was the last I ever saw of him. The next thing I know'd I was sittin' in a fine passenger car and the train was stoppin' at the station. My arm didn't hurt or nothin'. My clothes was all clean. The conductor said I was at my stop, so I got off. It was a real nice place. A real nice place. Jus' like a regular town, but everythin' and everybody was nice - nobody fussin' at you. Ain't nobody sick, nobody hurtin'. I don't know how, but everybody knowed my name and I knowed theirs. Most of them folks don't speak English, but, I can understand them anyway an' they can understand me. People's always askin' you to stay for supper. Plenty of kids to play with. A lady named Halina had a room all fixed up for me. She's real nice. That's where I stay. I bet she would let you stay there too, or you could get your own place and I could stay with you. You see Lonnie, that's why I come back. To get you. To take you back with me. All you need's a ticket and that engine. Lonnie, don't you see how nice it'll be. We can always be together. That's why I come back to get you. Please Lonnie, you got to come."

At that moment Pogo, whose curiosity had been aroused by the voices coming from inside the shed, poked his head in the door.

"Is that your dog?" Vonnie asked.

"Yes."

Pogo ambled up to Vonnie, tail wagging, and softly rubbed his muzzle against the boy's leg.

"I bet he can come too," he said, reaching down and patting Pogo's head, "if that's what's worryin' you. All he needs is a ticket. I got to go now, can't stay any longer, arm's hurtin' bad. Got to get back."

With that, he was gone. Lonelle struggled up to his feet. He tucked the tender under his arm and cradled the station to his chest. He looked at Pogo. "Are you seein' this too?" Pogo wagged his tail. "Humphh. I'll take that as a yes. Come on, let's git outta here."

A few days passed since the encounter with Jorge had set his otherwise placid existence on its ear. The afternoon was wearing on as Lonelle sat at the big table sipping sweet tea and staring out the window. Pogo, lying in his usual spot, perked up his ears. "What is it?" Lonelle asked, reaching down and stroking the dog's head. Pogo got up and worked his way through the house to the front door and yelped. "What you want now?" Lonelle called out. "I jus' took you out." Pogo pressed his nose against the door just as the front doorbell rang. "What now?" Lonelle grumbled. Pogo let out a low growl. The doorbell rang again. Probable the Jehovah's Witnesses. He slowly got up from his chair. The bell rang one more time before he made it to the door. He peered through the sidelight to see two police officers standing on the porch. Beyond them, storm clouds were gathering on the horizon. Can't be no good. He unlatched the door and stepped out. "What ya'll want?" he asked.

"Good afternoon sir," the officer closest to the door offered. "I am officer Talberg and this is Officer Perez," he said gesturing to the other officer. "May we have a word with you?"

"What ya'll want?"

"We're going through the neighborhood looking for a child that's gone missing," said the officer, holding up a photograph. "Have you seen this child?"

"Let me have a look." The officer held the photograph closer. Lonelle recognized Jorge immediately. "What's goin' on?"

"Neighbors reported screaming and gunshots from the mother's apartment. The mother and an adult male were found on the scene dead of gunshot wounds. Neighbors said this child was also living in the apartment, but has not been seen. We don't know of any relatives in the area, so we are going house to house looking for him."

"Mebbe I've seen him around here a while back, but not lately."

"Thank you sir," the officer said handing Lonelle a business card. "If you see him, please give us a call."

"What'll happen when you find him?"

"He will be given over to child protective services."

"Well, where was they when all this happened?" Lonelle barked.

"Thank you sir. If you see anything, please notify us."

Lonelle glared at the officers as they left the porch. He flung the door shut and threw the latch. Pogo stood at the opening into the hallway wagging his tail. Lonelle passed him by without so much as a nod on his way back to the kitchen. Pogo followed. Instead of taking up his usual spot under the big table, he worked his way over to the kitchen door and yelped. "Be quiet," Lonelle admonished. Pogo yelped again. "Can't a body sit in peace without dogs barkin' and doorbells ringin'?" Pogo pushed at the door sash with his nose, causing it to bump against the jamb. "Alright, alright, hold on. I'll let you out, but don't count on me lettin' you back in. I'm gonna sit here and finish my tea, if you don't mind." He opened the door and Pogo hop, step, stepped as fast as he could straight out to the shed. What now? Pogo put his nose up close to the door and barked, then turned his head and looked at Lonelle. He repeated this again and again until Lonelle grabbed the keys from the hook and set out for the shed.

"What's goin' on here?" Lonelle asked, as he unlocked the shed door. He pulled it open carefully, expecting some varmint to come scampering out. Instead, he heard soft whimpering coming from a dark corner of the shed. He moved forward through the boxes he had left on the floor and peered into the shadows. Jorge sat huddled, face buried in drawn-up knees.

His right arm covered his head, while his left hung by his side. He was sobbing. Lonelle navigated the boxes and reached down to the child. "Now, now, no need for you to be afraid no more," he said softly. "Come on now, lets us get up to the house before someone finds us down here. The police is lookin' for you. Can't let them find you, can we? No sir, got to get you up to the house." He reached down and touched Jorge's shoulder. The boy cried out in pain. "What's this here? You hurt?" Jorge moaned as he drew his head lower into his chest. "Hor-Hay, it's me, Lonelle. Don't be afraid. I ain't gonna let nothin' happen to you. Now, let me take a look at you," he said, bending down to the crying child. Jorge lifted his head enough for Lonelle to see his bruised face. "My God, my God, what happen' to you?" Jorge looked down and continued his sobbing. "I know you're hurt an' scared, but you can't stay out here. Come on with me. You'll be safe up to the house and we'll find you a soft place to lie down. Won't you come on?"

While Lonelle had been coaxing Jorge, Pogo had picked his way through the boxes. He let out a soft whimper and gently licked the child's exposed cheek. Jorge looked up, taking a break from his sobbing. He reached out and patted Pogo on the head. "See there," Lonelle cooed, "Ol' Pogo is worried about you too. Now we all can't stay out here, so come on up to the house." Lonelle took Jorge's hand. "If I could carry you, I would, but with these old leg braces and all, I jus' can't, so's you'll have to help out." He held Jorge's had while he got to his feet and then guided him through the boxes until they were standing outside the shed. Lonelle paused to lock the door then said, "Let's git."

The last rays of the sun were peeking over the treetops as Pogo led the trio slowly up the gravel path to the house. They stopped in the kitchen long enough for Lonelle to wash Jorge's face and fix a cold compress. Then, they headed for the spare room where Lonelle helped Jorge up on the bed. Lonelle stood by the bed until Jorge fell asleep, then went into the living room and flopped into his easy chair to figure what to do next. He was weary and his eyes felt heavy. Lonelle felt a nudge on his shoulder.

"Lonnie, wake up."

"Is that you, Vonnie?"

"Yes."

"Prove it or let me be."

"You want me to prove it's me? Ain't I enough proof, jus' standin' here talking to you. Ain't your eyes no good? You can't see it's me? What kind of foolishness is this? Here I am, arm hurtin' to all git out, when I could be sittin' pretty, having a fine supper with Miss Halina, an' you wants proof."

"Yes. So get on with it." Lonelle demanded.

"Look, if I can prove I'm real, will you come back with me?"

"Mebbe. But, I sure won't do it if you don't try. So's get busy or quit wastin' my time. I got important things to work out here, an' I ain't got time for dreams if they ain't real."

"How?"

"Well, that's for you to figure out."

Vonnie thought for a while before he answered. "Alright, I'm ready."

"OK, but you only get one chance. If you don't convince me first time out, then you're outta here, agreed?"

"Agreed." Vonnie paused. "I guess by now you have figured out from what I told you that my train an' your train are one in the same. Now, you could say since you already had that old train, that it could jus' be part of the dream, but I didn't tell you where the old man kept the wooden box, did I? Well, he kept it in the station," Vonnie said, walking over to the table where Lonelle had placed it. "See, the roof slides back." He lifted the wooden box out and handed it to his brother. "Go ahead and open it, you'll find the record book and tickets inside."

"Well, I'll be," Lonelle muttered. He examined the box. It was inscribed with foreign words. Inside, he found a canvas-bound book. It contained page after page of what appeared to be names and dates. On the last page, near the bottom he found the last entry. It read: 'Vonelle Turner, 15.10.1950 r'. He looked at Vonnie and stammered, "I . . . I don't know what to say. . . "

"Don't say nothin' till I'm finished. An' what about the gold key. No, it ain't in the box. No, he kept it in the tender. Just shift the coal box back and you'll find the key underneath."

Lonelle picked up the tender from the stand next to his chair and carefully pushed on the coal box. It slid back about an inch revealing a gold key in a compartment below. "Well, I'll be," he whispered. He took it out and set the tender back, then picked up the engine. With trembling fingers, he inserted the key into the slot on top of the boiler. It slid in smoothly.

"Don't wind it 'til you're ready," Vonnie warned. "Do you believe me now?"

"Did you say more than one person could ride the train at the same time?"

"Don't know. Look in the book and see if there are multiple entries with the same date."

Lonelle thumbed through the book. "Looks like they is."

"Well, my bet is that more than one can go on the same ride."

"Can dogs go too?"

"Don't see why not if they got a ticket. What you got in mind?"

"Jus' that more than me might want a ride on that train."

"Well, I think that whole place where I end'd up mus' be made up from folks that needed a ride on that train. I guess a few more won't make a bit of difference."

"You ever see Mr. K where you're at?" Lonelle asked.

"No, if he took the train, his name would be in there after me. You see his name in there?"

"No, you's the last one in the book. He musta died before he made it."

"That's a shame. He was a good man."

The two remained silent for some time before Vonnie spoke. "Lonnie."

"Yeah."

"You believe me now?"

'Yeah."

"Then you gonna use a ticket?"

"Yeah."

"OK. I got to go. I got to get back before you get on the train. Got to be there to meet you an' show you 'round. I won't be back after this. Don't forget to write your name in the book. An' don't forget your ticket. Remember, you can't ride the train without a ticket. Don't forget. OK?"

"Yes, I got it. Jus' need a little time to get things ready."

Vonnie faded away. Pogo sniffed the space where he had been standing, then turned his head and looked quizzically at Lonelle. "I don't know where he went," he responded. "I guess we'll know soon enough, won't we? We best be leavin' before I thinks myself out of this. Hey, I jus' thought of somethin'. Do you think you'll get a new leg when we get there? Wouldn't that be nice."

Lonelle set the book on the stand and sifted through the papers remaining in the box. They were mostly yellowed newspaper clippings. He examined them closely. They crumbled in his fingers and were definitely not from American papers. A good many featured photographs of people moving along country roads in long lines. They trudged on foot and rode in battered horse carts. The carried flimsy suitcases and tattered bundles. All had the look of despair in their faces. The word 'NAZISTA' would appear now and again in the text that accompanied the photos. Lonelle could only guess that these were war refugees. He lifted the last of the loose clippings and other papers from the box. He had been searching for anything with the word BILIT on it. There at the bottom, he found what he was looking for. He paused for a moment, focusing intently on his discovery.

"Yes, yes," he whispered excitedly. "Come on dog. We got work to do." He placed the book back in the wooden box, picked up the engine and started off for the spare room. Pogo followed, tail wagging. Jorge lay fast asleep on the bed. Lonelle removed the compress and touched him gently on the forehead.

"Wake up Hor-Hay," he whispered. Jorge opened his eyes. "That's good. We got somethin' to talk about. Are you listenin'?" Jorge nodded. "I got real bad news for you. I think your mama's dead. Mebbe you already knew that. If not, wish I didn't have to tell you like this, but there jus' ain't no way to deliver bad news 'cept say it right out. If I could change the way things is, I would." Tears welled up in Jorge's eyes. "Yes, go ahead, let them tears come. I know how bad it gets when your mama dies. I wasn't much older than you when my mama passed away. You feels all alone, an' scared like you ain't never gonna make it, but you will. Me and Pogo is here, and we gonna see you're taken care of. You listenin'?" Jorge nodded. "That's good, 'cause I got more to tell you. I think your arm it is broke for sure an' we jus' can't leave you here without doin' nothin'. As I see it, we only got two ways to go. We'll take you to doctor, in which case you will eventually end up with child protective services. If that happens, we prob'ly won't never see you again. I don't think that's a good thing for you, an' I don't think you would think so once you got there. Or, we'll get you to a place where everythin' is better than it is here. There won't be no storm clouds, jus' sunshine. You won't be hurtin' no more neither. There won't be no yellin' or hittin'. Ever'body will be real nice. An' you won't be alone. My brother Vonnie is already there waitin'. He's jus' about your age. You and him would get along jus' fine. Now, we ain't got much time. What you think?" Jorge nodded. "That's good. Now you stay still. This won't take long."

Lonelle pulled a chair up close to the bed. He placed the engine and the box on the mattress between himself and Jorge. He pulled the book from the box and retrieved a pencil from the drawer in the nightstand. "Now how you spell your name again?"

"J-O-R-G-E," he responded. He watched Lonelle move the pencil across the page of the book, pausing now and then while he closed his eyes and took a measured breath.

"There we go, ever'thin' recorded official like," Lonelle said, closing the book and setting it in his lap. He reached into the box and pulled out a stub of paper. "This here is your ticket. It's real important. You got to keep it with you always. Don't never let it get away from you. Understand?" Jorge nodded. Lonelle tucked the ticket into the pocket of Jorge's shirt and gave it a soft pat. "There you go. We only got one more thing to do before the trip starts." He picked up the engine, pointing to the gold key protruding from the top of the boiler. "I found it. All's we got to do is wind this thing up and the train ride begins. What do you say, you ready?" Jorge nodded again, brushing away the tears that trickled down his puffy cheeks. Lonelle turned the key with trembling fingers. The key worked smoothly within the mechanism, clicking as the spring within the engine tightened. When it would turn no more, Lonelle placed the train on the bed. "Now, all you got to do is jus' push this little bell," he said to Jorge, touching it lightly with his finger. Jorge reached over and placed his finger tentatively on the bell. "Go on now, ain't nothin' goin' to happen lessen' you push it. Go ahead." Jorge pushed. Lonelle watched as he faded away.

Jorge marveled at the richly decorated passenger coach. A whistle blew as the train came to a stop in front of the ornate station building. A plume of steam shot out from underneath the train as it came to a full stop. The conductor, dressed in a blue uniform with red piping and shiny brass buttons, stopped at his seat. "Ticket please." Jorge fished out the ticket Lonelle had placed in his shirt pocket and showed it to the conductor. Bending down for a closer look, he studied it for a moment, then said, "Ahhh, OSTATNI BILET - the last ticket. This is your stop, Jorge. The end of the line." He pointed to the door at the front of the car. Jorge slid across the seat and walked to the doorway. He paused at the top step, looking out at the station and the bustling town beyond, then hopped down. The conductor followed. Vonnie stood on the broad platform with a broad smile on his face.

"Hey, Jorge, I'm Vonnie, how you doin'?"

"Jus' fine."

"Come on, Miss Halina's fixin' supper. Pierogies, I bet. Bet you ain't never had none; but they's real good. How's the shoulder?"

"Feels good," Jorge said, flexing his arm. He held out the ticket still clutched in his hand. "The conductor said this is the last ticket. I thought we were all coming here together - I mean Mr. Lonelle, Pogo, and me. They must've decided to stay."

"I don't think any of us ever had a say in the matter. I think it was always the train that decided who needed to come here and who was strong 'nough to stay. Come on, let's git back before supper gets cold."

Behind them, the train exhaled its final breath of steam and faded from sight.

Lonelle sat motionless, staring at the empty bed. A moment later, the train blinked out of sight. He felt around on the bed where it had been. There was nothing to indicate it had ever been there. Pogo stepped forward and placed his muzzle next to Lonelle's hand.

"Well, I figured Hor-Hay would fly off somewhere, but I never 'spected the train to disappear." Pogo let out a mournful whimper. "Don't you tell me you wanted to go away on that train? Myself, I never really planned to go. Besides, there was only one space left in that book to write a name an' only one ticket left in that box. Figured Hor-Hay needed it more than me. I know Vonnie wanted us to come be with him real bad, but if that place really works like he says, he'll understand. Ever'thin' will turn out alright." He put his hand on Pogo's graying head. "Besides, what would you do with another leg? You're already smarter than all them other dogs," he laughed, brushing back a tear. Pogo wagged his tail. "That's what I thought you'd say."

SHATTER MAN[7]

Seth forced his body up from the table. Tugging on an old, stained, army trench coat, he peered out the front door window through the driving rain looking into each dark corner along the street outside. Stepping out, he searched from side to side, cold rain pelting his greasy, matted hair until rivulets of water ran into his bloodshot eyes. Convinced no one was lurking in the shadows, he bolted out the door in hopes to reach the crumbling tenement and then scramble up the stairs to his apartment before the rain soaked through his clothes. It had been coming down in torrents all afternoon overcoming the storm drains, filling the streets with turbid water to the curb line and above. Down the street to the left, a woman approached. His right foot, expecting to land on the curb's edge, overshot its mark throwing him headlong into swirling runoff.

An afternoon of gin already had his head spinning and the sudden fall coupled with the rude shock of cold water further disoriented him. The thick trench coat drank in the grey water, weighting him down. He flailed his arms and legs against an invisible hand while the suction of the storm water pulled his face against the storm grate. Lungs straining against his chest wall searched for air as blood pounded inside his skull. He kept his mouth clenched and pulled his arms close to his body, shaking hands placed flat against the grate below. The violent water gushed down through the mesh pinning him. Burning muscles leached the last molecules of oxygen from depleted blood in a futile attempt to lift his aching body out of the water. Mouth

---

[7] "Shatter Man" appeared on line in *This Dark Matter Black Friday Fiction*, 7/10/2015.

opening in the last gasp of a drowning man, the grey, gritty runoff flooded his mouth and throat.

A hard sharp slap to his back was not what he expected. He opened his eyes to see the wet sidewalk inches below. Raindrops spat the pitted concrete around him. Another hard blow came. Burning lungs purged the water he had inhaled. Vomit welled up in his throat, spewing to the concrete. He breathed in the odor of cheap gin and bile making him wretch again. Now on hands and knees, muscles twitching, his head pounding with dull pain. He took another breath, deeper and less trembling than the last.

"There you go." declared a woman's voice clear and strong above the noise of the driving rain and traffic, "Can you sit up?"

Seth swung around sitting on his left hip, extending a weak arm to steady his trembling body. He looked up to see the young woman who had been walking up the street staring intently into his bleary eyes.

"That was a close call." she said kneeling down beside him. "Have you got your breath yet?"

Seth coughed, he could feel mealy bits of vomit clinging to his teeth and lips. He sucked saliva from beneath his tongue and spit violently. Then, a deep rattling cough brought up more water which he expelled as searing pain gripped his throat and lungs. After a few painful gasps for air he mumbled, "Yeah, yeah."

"Let's get you inside.' She said grabbing his right arm and standing up.

Wobbly, he stood up while his rescuer snaked an arm around his waist guiding him toward the door from which he had just stumbled. As they moved slowly toward the shelter of the tavern doorway, Seth stopped to let the spinning in his head subside and cast a furtive, searching look all around. Seeing nothing, he let a soft growl ooze out from his chest and turned back toward the door. She pulled on the worn brass handle of the weather beaten door as Seth shuffled in, shivering from the cold and the remnants of gin in his stomach. It was a sad, desolate space filled with booths and tables in various states of disrepair. She started across the scuffed black and white tile floor for the nearest booth, but Seth pulled her to a small table by the window.

"This here's my spot." He said slumping in a well worn straight backed chair that creaked in protest. "Pull one uh them chairs over and sit down," he rasped pointing to a tattered chair at the adjoining table.

A single, stained light bulb hanging from a frayed cord overhead lit the area around the small table. He peeled off the dripping trench coat and let it fall over the chair back. He sat quietly for a few minutes hunched over, chest heaving as his lungs sought to recharge the oxygen in his blood. Droplets of water worked their way down his ruddy face hanging momentarily on his chin before dropping onto the grimy table. He used the time to examine the woman. Long black hair framed her pale, oval face. Eyes, black as obsidian, returned his gaze. Thin lips, pursed neither in a smile or a frown, revealed nothing about her.

"Guess you think you done sumpin' grand out there," he barked, pointing a shaky finger past her head toward the street. "Well, weren't nothin' of the kind. I was jest 'bout to get up outta that hole when you took a notion to stick your nose in my binness. I'da bin jus' fine, jus' fine. Hey Jerry," he shouted raising one finger, "Gimme one here!"

"Go on, you've had enough," growled the barkeep, "Why don't you go home and sleep it off. You're dripping all over the furniture."

"I ain't, an' my money is as green as anyone's. So, shut up and bring me one." He sat quietly glaring alternately between the woman and the rain soaked street outside until Jerry sauntered over with a tumbler of gin. Setting it on the table, he said, "That'll be three fifty."

Seth muttered as he dug into his pocket and laid three soggy ones and a handful of dimes and nickels on the table. Jerry scooped up the money and retraced his steps to the bar. Seth took a long drink from the tumbler and smacked it down on the table. A wry smile crept across his weathered face. "Wern't nuthin'. I know'd I'd be alright. Din't see no sign of 'im, nowhere. No offence girly, but it whad'nt my time. It was nice and all, you stopping like that, but it was no big thing. Whether or not you come along din't matter, it jus' whad'nt my time. No, din't see 'im; not at all."

"See who, Seth?"

"The Shatter Man, dammit. Don't you know nuttin?"

"Apparently not, who is this shatter man?"

Seth leaned forward bringing his face as close to the woman as he could. Then in a low, cracking voice began to recite a childhood poem:

"Shatter Man, Shatter Man be on your way.
You won't catch me in the dark on this day.
You hides in the rocks and behind the trees,
Thinkin' you can take whoever you please.

"Shatter Man, Shatter Man pass me on by.
If you steal me away, mama will cry.
Don't take me down there, where it's cold below.
Please not to the place where tha dead folk go.

"Shatter Man, Shatter Man I know what to do.
I know how to get tha better of you.
I'll always make sure I play in the light.
An' never go out in the dead of night."

Slamming his hand down hard on the table, he threw back his head and snorted, "That's 'im! The one that comes to git you. He hides in tha shatters and the dark places an' grabs you if you ain't lookin'. Then he takes you down below with all the dead folk. Most folks can't see 'im, or they don't want to see 'im, 'cause they's afraid they'll see him, and then know their time is up. But, I can see 'im. Been able to see 'im since I was jus' a kid. An' cause I can see 'im, I can beat 'im." Sitting back in the old chair, Seth cast a rheumy eye on the woman before bringing the tumbler to his lips and guzzling down the rest of the gin.

"First time I seen 'im, I was only 'bout ten years old. Cyrus Jacobs and I were playin' along Hobbs Run just up from the dam. We wasn't supposed to go to close to the dam cause the water would suck you right over in a heartbeat and trap you on the bottom where you'd drown. We was sitting on bank trying to see how far we could skip a stone along the dam before it got swallered up. That's when I seen 'im. The trees along the far bank were thick and hung low to the water. Not much sun could get through the leaves. But if you looked real hard an' squinted your eyes you could see things hidden over there. An' I seen 'im there all black in the shatters waving his long thin arm. He was beckonin' me to the water.

"Well, I jumped up an' started scramblin' to tha top of tha bank all the time yelling for Cyrus to run. It scared Cyrus so much that his feet got all tangled an' before you know it he slipped and fell back into the rushin' water. He screamed for help; but, as I turned back, I could see the Shatter Man waitin' in tha dark across the swirlin' muddy water. I know'd if I went down that bank he'd get me for sure. Cyrus kept screamin' out to me for help and flailing about tryin' to get back to the shore. I watched 'till he was swept o'er the dam. Then, it got all quiet 'cept for the swooshin' of the water. I watched for him to surface on tha other side, but he never did. I looked back across to the other bank. The Shatter Man was gone.

"I know'd then it didn't matter to the Shatter Man who died, just as long as somebody died. He got what he wanted. I got away. As for Cyrus, they found him three days later, about two miles downstream, hung up in a tangle of tree roots.

"From then on, I kept on tha lookout for tha Shatter Man. A few years later, I was walkin' down Charter Street with Jimmy Blackburn. It was late in the day and the shatters had began to fill in the shop doors and alley ways. I looked up ahead and seen 'im hiding in tha dark at the edge of tha alley. Din't waste no time. I grabbed Jimmie by tha arm an' pushed him between a coupl'a parked cars so's we could run away. Just as we stepped out into tha street, a big ol' panel truck appeared out of nowhere. I looked over my shoulder and saw tha Shatter Man jus waiting there for me. It only took a little shove in tha back and Jimmy tumbled right out in tha path of that truck. Tha driver hit tha brakes jus about tha time he hit Jimmy. Threw him fifteen feet in the air before he hit tha dirt with a lifeless thud. I looked back and seen tha Shatter Man was gone.

"I decided there and then that I'd never let tha Shatter Man get me. An' I ain't so far; though I've seen him plenty of times. Sometimes I got away on my own; sometimes, I had to see to it somebody took my place. No tellin' how many I give 'im in 'Nam.

Never got me though, then or now, never will. Hell, I'm gonna live forever."

He fumbled through the dripping pockets of his trench coat and pulled out a soggy pack of cigarettes. He looked inside the crumpled box as if he expected to find a dry smoke hiding somewhere. He glanced up at the woman. "You got a cigarette?"

"Don't you know those things will kill you?" she admonished.

"If I die, it won't be 'cause of a little tar and nicotine. Anyways, like I said I'm gonna live forever."

"I doubt that. You'll live a long time; but, I think you'll wish you were dead before it's over."

"Now you're talkin' nonsense, girly."

"Really? Let's suppose your shatter man is just another bogyman from a child's poem. Life and death are a balancing act. Each day, you get up and wait to see which way the scales will tip. When it's your time to die, you are supposed to die. And when you do, there is no shatter man there. Just death. Death in any form it chooses. Death as relentless as rain drops washing away a mountain over the ages until it becomes a pebble. Seth, you've spent your life cheating the scales, setting up others to die in your place. If there is a shatter man, it's surely you, because you've shattered the life of every person you allowed to die in your stead; or, worse yet, killed because you were afraid to accept that your time was up. You've shattered their lives and the lives of the ones who loved them. Seth, that's a big load of misery and pain to carry around and you have a long way to carry it before you die."

Seth glowered at the woman and fumed, "You better get outta here before I do something you won't like."

"You've been doing that for some time now," she hissed pushing back from the table, "see you around." She shot him an icy stare before throwing the door open and disappearing into the driving rain.

"An' don't come back!" He bellowed rising up from his chair, pounding his fists on the table. The empty gin tumbler tipped over, rolled off the table and crashed to the tiled floor below.

"Alright you crazy fool," barked Jerry, reaching under the bar, retrieving an old battered night stick. "Get the hell out of here you stinking gin sot before I call the cops or better yet split that empty skull of yours!"

Seth fished a couple of soggy bills out of his pocket and tossed them on the floor as he struggled into his wet trench coat. "One's for the glass and give one to your mother for las' night." he spat.

Stumbling through the door, he staggered over to the curb eyeing the swirling water. Putting one hand on the street lamp to steady himself, he looked up just as a delivery truck swerved to miss the dark haired woman who had stepped out into the street. The truck careened along the slick pavement spewing out a blinding spray of oily water as it hurled headlong toward Seth. He couldn't move his gin heavy legs and the truck lunged head on, driving him across the sidewalk and crushing him against the pealing painted bricks of the tavern wall.

* * *

He did not expect to open his eyes and see shiny black and white tile below his face. The smell of antiseptics filled his nose. A soft cacophony of beeps, buzzes and whirs filled his ears. The tiles below his face started to slide away replaced by bare cream colored walls and eventually a stark white ceiling with a single glaring fluorescent light. All the while, stabbing pain afflicted his body. At first, he thought he was still trapped in his old army trench coat trapped under the truck hallucinating; but, soon realized he was completely cocooned inside of some contraption.

"There you go. These rotating beds are just the thing for unfortunates like you, stuck in a full body cast." The face of the woman with dark hair from the bar appeared in his field of vision. "Really hurts, doesn't it?"

Seth struggled to answer, but only a soft gurgle oozed painfully out of his throat.

Her black eyes burned down on him. "You've been in a coma for a week now; but, I just couldn't let you sleep away all this exquisite pain could I? Not to worry, Seth, eight months of torturous rehab and you should be up and about. Then you can resume your life. That's not much time, seeing how you're going to live forever.

"I've got to leave now, before your nurse shows up. I bet she'll be so happy to see you have regained consciousness. Don't worry though, I'll keep in touch. One question before I go: Was it Teddy O'Leary who died in the fire your senior year?"

Again, Seth attempted to answer; but, only manage a sound reminiscent of a cat coughing up a fur ball.

"Oh I forgot," she cooed, "you won't be able to speak for another month. Don't worry though; once you're out of here, we'll catch up on old times."

ABOUT THE AUTHOR

Paul Stansbury is a life long native of Kentucky. Now retired, he lives in Danville, Kentucky. He is the owner of Sheppard Press. In addition to *Inversion - Not Your Ordinary Stories,* he is the author of *Down By the Creek – Ripples and Reflections,* both published by Sheppard Press. His novelette, *Little Green Men?* was published by The Society of Misfit Stories.

His stories have appeared in the following print anthologies:

- "A Game Of Tag" and "Dark Meat" appeared in Brief Grislys published by Apocryphile Press
- "Sigaforgas" appeared in Neo-Legends To Last A Deathtime published by KY Story
- "The Ghost Eye" appeared in Frightening published by SEZ Publishing,
- "Takers" appeared in Out of the Cave published by MacKenzie Publishing,
- "Phantasmal" appeared in In Media Res, Stories From the In-Between published by Writespace Houston
- "Under the Wolf Moon" appeared in Nocturnal Natures published by Zimbell House Publishing.
- "Spirit Painter" appeared in Book 3: 30 Authors-30 Stories published by Flash Fiction Magazine
- "Exiled" appeared in See Through My Eyes: A Ghost Mystery Anthology published by Fantasia Divinity Magazine"
- Selkie Cove" appeared in Mirrors and Lakes published by Owls Ink

His work has also appeared in a variety of on-line publications. His poetry has appeared in The Rising Phoenix Review, Young Ravens Literary Review, Strange Poetry and Kentucky Monthly.

He is a contributing writer for the Danville Advocate Messenger Newspaper.

BOOKS FROM SHEPPARD PRESS

Down By The Creek – Ripples and Reflections by Paul Stansbury
ISBN 978-0-9986516-0-6 paperback
ISBN 978-0-9986516-1-3 e-book

Inversion – Not Your Ordinary Stories by Paul Stansbury
ISBN 978-0-9986516-3-7 paperback
ISBN 978-0-9986516-4-4 e-book

By George – A Collection Of Childhood Experiences and Anecdotes by George Herbert Stansbury, Jr.
ISBN 978-0-9986516-2-0 paperback

Sheppard Press